By Karen Erickson

The Wildwood Series
Ignite
Smolder
Torch

Torch

THE WILDWOOD SERIES

KAREN ERICKSON

AVONIMPULSE
An Imprint of HarperCollins Publishers

Excerpt from *The Virgin and the Viscount* copyright © 2016 by Charis Michaels.

Excerpt from *Love On My Mind* copyright © 2016 by Tracey Livesay.

Excerpt from *Here and Now* copyright © 2016 by Cheryl Etchison Smith.

EPub Edition AUGUST 2016 ISBN: 9780062441225

Print Edition ISBN: 9780062441232

Chapter One

WREN GALLAGHER WASN'T the type to drown her sorrows in alcohol, but tonight seemed as good a time as any to start.

"Another Malibu and pineapple, Russ," she said to the bartender, who gave her a look before nodding reluctantly. She'd known Russell Fry since she was a kid. Went to school with his daughter Amelia, who'd moved the hell out of Wildwood the minute she graduated high school. She'd received a full scholarship to some fancy Ivy League college and never looked back.

Many times over the last few years, she thought of Amelia. And envied her tremendously.

She'd gotten out.

And Wren hadn't.

Not that Wildwood was a bad place. She was happy here. She had a great job as a bookkeeper for various businesses around town, plus she'd invested in her friend

Delilah's dance studio. She had her family. She had her friends…friends who were all pairing off and finding love. All she could find was the bottom of an empty glass at a bar on a Monday night.

Woe is me and all that jazz. She'd roll her eyes at herself if she could guarantee it wouldn't make her head spin. She was sort of spinning already, despite her internal promise not to overdo it.

"That's your third drink," Russ said gruffly as he plunked the fresh glass in front of her.

She grabbed it and took a long sip from the skinny red straw. It was her third drink because the first two weren't potent enough. She didn't even feel that drunk. But how could she tell Russ that when he was the one mixing her drinks? "And they're equally delicious," she replied with a sweet smile.

He scowled at her, his bushy eyebrows threaded with gray hairs seeming to hang low over his eyes. "You all right, Wren?"

"I'm fine." She smiled, but it felt incredibly false, so she let it fade before taking another sip of her drink. No way could she tell this old man she'd known forever all her troubles. He'd tell her mother, who'd tell her father, and then they'd give her a call, asking her to come over so they could "talk." Forget it.

Forget. It.

Her problems were hers and hers alone. Plus, they sounded ridiculously selfish when she voiced them out loud. People lost their jobs, marriages broke up, children got bad grades and failed school, people were diagnosed with fatal diseases, for God's sake. What did she have to complain about? That she was feeling lonely? That maybe she felt the teeniest bit…stuck?

Yeah, she'd remained in her hometown versus running off to the big city, which had been her original after-high-school-graduation dream. She'd wanted to escape her tiny life, her family, all of it, but that never happened. She stayed home instead and worked and played and dealt with her family.

So her dad was a jerk. So her mom was a doormat. She still loved them. Her brothers were a pain in her ass, but she knew without a doubt if she asked any one of them—and she had three—for help, they'd drop everything to be there for her. No questions asked. That was nice. That fact alone made her feel safe.

And most of the time, she liked feeling safe.

She had good friends. Two best friends who each happened to be dating one of her brothers. What were the odds? Harper and West were serious. Lane finally came around and he was now in a full-blown relationship with Delilah. They even said they loved each other out loud. In front of other people and everything.

It kind of blew Wren's mind.

Oh, and it depressed her. A lot.

Sighing, she pushed the wimpy straw out of the way and brought the glass to her lips, chugging the drink in a few long swallows. Polishing it off like a pro, she wiped her damp lips with the back of her hand as she set the glass down on the bar. Her head spun a little bit and she blinked hard, pleased to finally experience the effects of the alcohol swimming in her veins.

A low whistle sounded behind her and she went still, her breath trapped in her lungs. No way was that whistle meant for her. It was a typical Monday night at the bar. Well, what she assumed was typical considering she didn't normally hang out here on Monday nights. She was literally the only female in the place beyond the waitress who had worked here forever. Helen was sixty-five with an old-fashioned beehive hairstyle that was dyed an artificially bright red. So she sort of didn't count in Wren's book.

"Trying to get drunk, Dove?"

That too-amused, too-arrogant voice was disappointingly familiar. Her shoulders slumping, she glanced to her right to watch as Tate Warren settled his too-perfect butt onto the barstool next to hers, a giant smile curving his too-sexy mouth as he looked her up and down. Her body heated everywhere his eyes landed, and she frowned.

Ugh. She hated him. His new favorite thing was to call her every bird name besides her own. It drove her crazy, and he knew it. It didn't help that they ran into each other all the time. The town was too small and their circle of mutual friends—and family members—even smaller.

Tate worked at Cal Fire with her brothers Weston and Holden. He was good friends with West and her oldest brother, Lane, so they all spent a lot of time together when they could. But fire season was in full swing, and Tate had been at the station the last time they all got together.

She hadn't missed him either. Not one bit.

At least, that's what she told herself.

"What are you doing here?" Her tone was snottier than she intended and he noticed. His brows rose, surprise etching his very fine, very handsome features.

He was seriously too good-looking for words. Like Abercrombie & Fitch type good-looking. With that pretty, pretty face and shock of dark hair and the finely muscled body and *oh, shit*, that smile. Although he wasn't flashing it at her right now like he usually did. Nope, not at all.

"I'm assuming you're looking to get drunk alone tonight? I don't want to get in your way." He started to stand and she reached out, resting her hand on his forearm to stop him.

And oh wow, his skin was hot. And firm. As in, the boy's got muscles. Erm, the man. Tate could never be mistaken for a boy. He was all man. One hundred percent delicious, sexy man…

"Don't go," she said, her eyes meeting his. His brows went up until they looked like they could reach his hairline, and she snatched her hand away, her fingers still tingling where she touched him.

Whoo boy, that wasn't good. Could she blame it on the alcohol?

Tate settled his big body back on the barstool, ordering a Heineken when Russ asked what he wanted. "You all right, Bird?" His voice was low and full of concern, and her heart ached to say something. Admit her faults, her fears, and hope for some sympathy.

But she couldn't do that. Couldn't make a fool of herself in front of Tate. She'd never hear the end of it. It was bad enough how he always managed to give her a hard time.

So she'd let the "Bird" remark go. At least he hadn't called her Cuckoo or Woodpecker. "Having a bad day," she offered with a weak smile, lifting her ice-filled glass in a toasting gesture. At that precise moment, Russ delivered Tate's beer and he raised it as well, clinking the green bottle against her glass.

"Me too," Tate murmured before he took a drink, his gaze never leaving hers.

Wren stared at him in a daze. How come she never noticed how green his eyes were before? They matched the beer bottle, which proved he didn't have the best taste in beer, but she'd forgive him for that.

But yes. They were pretty eyes. Kind eyes. Amused eyes. Laughing eyes. Sexy eyes.

She tore her gaze away from his, mentally beating herself up. He chuckled under his breath, and she wanted to beat him up too. Just before she ripped off his clothes and had her way with him...

Oh, jeez. Clearly she was drunker than she thought.

TATE CONCENTRATED ON drinking his beer, trying his best not to look in the direction of the beautiful girl who always acted like she hated him. But it was proving difficult, considering she was sitting so close. As in, he-could-smell-her close. She'd-actually-voluntarily-touched-him close.

Even kissing close.

Not that he could kiss Wren. She'd probably sock him in the mouth if he ever tried. She'd seemed irritated by him from the very first moment they met. He had no idea what happened, what exactly made her act that way toward him, but her rude behavior became a sort of game. He'd even named the game, just for fun.

How fast can I piss off Wren?

Pretty damn fast was always the answer. He loved giving her a hard time, considering she always reacted so strongly, like he was the bane of her existence. Calling her whatever bird species came to mind instead of her actual name? Pure genius on his part. She hated it.

He loved it.

More like he loved driving her crazy.

If he was being truthful, he loved her name too. It was pretty. Unique. Much like the woman herself.

Yeah, that thought got him nowhere.

All his life, women had never been much of a challenge. He'd smile, he'd flirt, and the next thing he knew, they were giving him the eye. Letting him know in no uncertain terms that they were up for anything. Lucky for them, he was always up for anything too. But he kept it simple and easy. No complications, no commitment, no unnecessary emotions getting in the way. He liked it that way.

No, he fucking *loved* it that way. Commitment was for sissies.

So his new friend West had fallen hard for Harper Hill. Like he could blame the man. She looked like someone who'd take care of you and rock your world, all at once.

And Lane and Delilah had recently taken a step in the commitment direction too. He could get on board with that as well. Though Delilah scared the crap out of him, truth be told. Why, he wasn't sure. Wren should scare the crap out of him too. She was a little mean. A lot grumpy. Always giving him shit. Treating him like he was a big joke.

That's why it blew his mind how attracted he was to Wren when she acted like he drove her crazy. And he sort of did—drive her crazy. Maybe he hadn't left the best impression on her when he first moved to Wildwood. He'd been extra flirtatious. Extra…man-whorish? Isn't that what Wren told him that one time last summer when she found him in the women's bathroom at this very bar? His hands on some random tourist's chest and his tongue down her throat?

The look of disgust on Wren's face when she saw them together had made him feel bad. Guilty even. And he never did guilty. He wasn't one to let someone else's judgment dictate his actions.

Yet with Wren…after that one slightly scandalous moment last summer, he'd cleaned up his act. Well, a little bit. He at least became more discreet.

Truthfully? He wanted to get discreet with Wren. But every time he got close to her, she rolled her eyes and gave him endless crap over something fairly menial. What was her deal?

Worse, what was *his* deal when it came to Wren? For some strange reason he wanted her approval. He wanted her to like him, which was just…

Odd.

He normally didn't give a shit what people thought of him.

"When did your eyes get so green?"

He turned to stare at her, stunned by her question. Stunned even more by the dreamy expression on her face as she stared at him like she wanted to...gobble him up?

"What did you just say?" he asked carefully.

"Your eyes." She waved a hand in their general direction, and he couldn't help but let his gaze drop to her chest. She had a nice one, and he was always trying to sneak a peek. Now he just blatantly stared. "They're so green. Like your beer."

Jerking his gaze away from her tits, Tate grabbed the bottle and held it to his lips, taking a drink before he said, "The beer isn't green, Blue Jay. But the bottle is."

"You know what I mean." She waved her hand again, nearly smacking him in the jaw. "They're very sparkly." When he looked at her like she was crazy, she clarified, "Your eyes."

"They are?"

"Oh, yeah." She nodded, a giggle slipping past her lips. "Sparkly and green and so very pretty."

His entire body went warm, and his dick twitched. Huh. He'd had women tell him he had nice eyes. His mother had always raved about his eyes when he was a kid, even going so far as to force him to wear green shirts to "bring out the color in your eyes." This wasn't an unusual compliment.

No, what was unusual was his reaction to it. Maybe it was the way Wren watched him. Or the way she seemed to sway toward him as she spoke, like there was a magnetic force pulling them closer together. One she couldn't fight no matter how hard she tried.

"Thank you," he said, his voice low as he contemplated her, skimming the length of her before his gaze returned to hers. "You have very, very pretty eyes too."

Those very pretty eyes widened in surprise and she pressed her lips together, blinking rapidly. "Seriously?"

Tate nodded, wondering why she'd doubt him. Then again, she would, what with the way they gave each other endless grief. "Definitely. Hasn't anyone ever told you that before?"

"Not really. You certainly haven't."

"I just did," he reminded her, making her roll her eyes.

Ah, there was the Wren he knew.

She shrugged and turned toward the bar, grabbing her drink, disappointment written all over her face when she realized it was empty. "I should probably go."

"You wouldn't let me leave," he pointed out. "So I think you should stay. Keep me company."

"What are you doing here anyway?"

That was a good question. Sitting at home on his first full day off in what felt like forever, he'd been bored. Restless. So he'd hopped in his SUV and drove around town, but he soon got bored with that too. He didn't know what he wanted, what he was looking for, but the moment he entered the bar and saw the back of Wren's head, he knew it was her.

And his night got magically better. Just like that.

"Bored," he answered truthfully. "Thought I'd stop by and grab a drink."

She gave him a look. "Really? Don't tell me this is your deep dark secret. That you come hang out here on your nights off and drink yourself into oblivion."

"Never." He polished off the beer and nodded at Russ, the old bartender who also happened to own the place. "Bring the lady another one too," he told him.

Russ frowned. "I don't think that's a good idea."

That earned another eye roll from Wren. "Come on, Russ. You're not my dad."

"Thank God for that, child." Russ shook his head as he approached them. "She's already had three," he told Tate.

"And I'd like another, please." She hiccupped, bouncing on the stool, and Tate couldn't help but think she looked kinda cute. And kinda inebriated. "Come on, Russ. Don't be such a party pooper," she whined.

"I'll take care of her," Tate said quietly, his words for Russ only. "Make sure she gets home safe."

"You sure about that? I've known this girl since she was three and liked to eat dirt pies for dessert." The pointed look Russ sent him was loud and clear. He'd entrust Wren to Tate's keeping, but he'd better keep his hands to himself.

Wren groaned and shook her head. "Why would you go and say that?" Her gaze met Tate's, and she seemed to be trying her best to look sincere. "I swear I never ate dirt."

The harrumph noise Russ made as he went to mix her a fresh drink said otherwise.

"Your secret's safe with me, Seagull." Chuckling, Tate reached out and tucked a loose strand of hair behind her ear, his fingers lingering on her soft skin. She sucked in an audible breath, her blue eyes going wide, her lips parting. They were pink. And damp. Her cheeks were rosy—he'd bet money that was alcohol induced—and her gaze seemed to—again—gobble him up. Like she enjoyed his touch. Like she wanted more of it.

He had to be seeing things. Reading something into nothing. No way did Wren Gallagher *want* him.

Did she?

Chapter Two

TATE JUST TOUCHED her. Like, in a sweet, caring manner. Boyfriends tucked hair behind their girl's ear. Irritating dudes who called her Seagull and thought it was funny did not.

Wren frowned, hating that he acted all sweet and then called her Seagull. How dumb was that? They were the scavengers of the bird species. They ate garbage. The lost ones who somehow couldn't find the ocean and made their home at the next best thing they could find—a landfill.

Yeah. Seagulls sucked.

And so did Tate Warren.

Though she was sort of lying. He didn't suck. Not really. He was being nice to her. Made sure she got another drink, which was delicious, though this time around she drank it a little slower because wow, she was buzzing hard. She kept pace with Tate as he sipped from his beer, admiring how the strong column of his throat moved when he swallowed. And the way his black T-shirt clung to his shoulders and stretched across his chest.

She'd seen that chest bare, the time they all met for a barbecue by the lake a few weeks ago. He'd been in bright blue board shorts and nothing else and, um, wow. She could still remember what he looked like that day. Little droplets of water had clung to his bare, tanned skin. She'd been tempted to lick every last one of those drops and see if he tasted as good as he looked…

Wren slapped her hands against her cheeks. Hard. So hard Tate's head whipped around, and he stared at her like she'd lost her mind. She sort of had, thinking such lusty thoughts about someone she really didn't like.

Really.

"Is my story so boring you had to slap yourself to wake up?" he asked, amusement lacing his deep voice.

"No, I just…" How was she going to explain herself? Forget it. She dropped her hands and smiled as politely as she could. "Carry on." He'd been telling her about a recent medical call where the old lady's cat had been stuck in a very tall pine tree and how she'd fully expected him to climb it and rescue her pet.

Typical firefighter fare she'd heard many times before, if she was being truthful. Her dad was a retired battalion chief. Her brothers worked at Cal Fire. She'd heard many a fire-related story over the years. They weren't that impressive. She didn't usually go gaga over a guy in uniform because, *hello*, most of the time they reminded her of her dad.

So yeah. Firefighters were no big deal. That meant *Tate* was no big deal. She needed to remember that.

Like, really remember it.

His gaze narrowed as he studied her for a quiet moment. He brought the bottle to his lips and finished off his beer. She followed suit and drank the last of her cocktail, setting the glass on the bar with a loud thump.

"I think it's time to take you home," he said.

She leaned back a little. "You're going to take me home?"

"Did you think you could drive yourself?" he asked incredulously.

"Um, I hadn't thought that far yet?"

"Exactly." She opened her mouth to protest, but he kept talking. "Someone could bring you by here tomorrow, right? So you can pick up your car?" He slid off the barstool and stood next to her, his hands sinking into the pockets of his cargo shorts, his expression expectant. "Or you could call me and I'll pick you up and—"

"No, no. I'm sure I can find someone who'll bring me. I've inconvenienced you enough." She hopped off the stool and tilted her head back, smiling up at him. He was very tall. And he smelled really good. Like spicy, clean man. She leaned in close, trying to take a subtle whiff, but she stumbled and nearly fell into him before he caught her. His hands on her shoulders, he held her away from him, his brows furrowed.

"You all right?" He bent his knees so he could gaze into her eyes and she knew. Right then she freaking *knew* that she wanted to kiss stupid Tate before the end of the night.

"I'm…great," she said, sounding a little breathless. Oh, yeah, she felt absolutely wonderful with his hands gripping her shoulders and the way he looked at her. Like he could see right through her, down to the very thoughts she was having about kissing him.

Hmm. Could he read her mind? She hoped not. Or maybe she hoped so because, hey, she wanted him to kiss her. Or she wanted to kiss him. Or whoever had the guts to make the first move because, wow, he had nice lips. His lower lip was full, and it looked tuggable. She'd gently bite down and give it a little tug with her teeth…

"You don't look so great," he said, his deep, very concerned voice breaking through her tumultuous thoughts. "You're kinda pale."

Fine. So her head was spinning. Was it because of him or the alcohol? Maybe both? "Seriously. I'm awesome." She took a step backward and his hands fell away from her, making her sad. She liked it when he touched her. "Ready to go? Wait, I need to pay."

"I already took care of it. Let's go." He took her by the arm, his fingers gently grasping her elbow as he steered her out of the bar. She said good-bye to Russ and waved at a few of the patrons, men she'd known for what felt like forever.

She was a little wobbly on her feet, and she was glad Tate had a hold of her as he escorted her out to the parking lot. That and she liked the way she felt when he touched her. Her head buzzed. Her blood heated. Her stomach swam with nerves and anticipation—of what, she wasn't actually sure, but wasn't that the best part?

That she didn't know what might happen when Tate took her home?

Her mind practically spun with the endless possibilities…

"Here we go," he said as they slowed down near his black SUV. He had a nice car. He had a nice everything, truth be told. And clearly she was drunk because she had her head tilted to the side so she could check out his nice ass. Totally rude. Totally blatant.

But she totally didn't care.

Wren started giggling, and she pressed her fingers against her lips to stifle the sound. But she couldn't stop it—or help it. She started laughing harder when Tate let go of her arm and opened the passenger side door.

"What's so funny?" he asked, that adorable frown of his making her melt a little inside. He was cute when he was frustrated.

"Nothing." She tried her best to look sincere but failed when a hiccup escaped her. "I'm, um…" She mentally searched for the right word.

"Drunk?" he offered, his frown evaporating and giving way to a smile. One of those I'll-take-care-of-you-even-though-you're-smashed-type smiles. Hmm, like maybe she was an idiot and he was losing patience dealing with her.

Uh-oh. Was he?

"Am I a pain?" she asked him once they were both settled inside his car. His scent lingered, and she breathed deep, savoring it. She could sit in his car forever and never get sick of smelling him.

Looking at him.

Her thoughts were…random. Definitely not normal. Tomorrow she'd probably go back to disliking him, but tonight she'd contemplate making a move on him. It was the alcohol talking. It made her bold. It made her stupid.

What would he do if she grabbed him?

She was leaning across the console when he finally said something.

"What do you mean?" He started the car and threw it into Reverse, glancing over his shoulder before his gaze met hers.

Up close, those pretty green eyes of his were extra intense. They sort of made her forget what she wanted to say. "Um, having to babysit me and drive me home. You probably have better things to do with your time."

"I don't mind."

"Uh-huh." That's what they all said. She'd been in this predicament before. Once one of Lane's friends had to take her home from a party after she'd passed out on the couch. He'd begrudged the situation the entire drive back to her place, grumbling under his breath how he wasn't getting paid to be a babysitter, so why was he being treated like one?

Ouch. The memory stung. Of course, she'd been all of twenty, and Lane had been furious when he caught her drinking. Like he didn't get drunk all the time before he turned legal age. Though her big brother was a pretty straight arrow. That's why they could always count on him to handle family stuff when it went south…

"Your brain is just a-workin' over there, isn't it?" Tate gently teased, bringing her back to the here and now. "Seriously, Robin. I don't mind driving you home. It's no big deal."

He was still calling her bird names, and it sucked. It sucked bad. She was tired of the other birds and the teasing and the pretend hate for each other. Though he never seemed to really hate her…more like she was the one who always acted like *she* hated *him*.

And she did. She so did. Because he made her want to do and say things she had no business wanting to do or say. He was a player—by his own admittance. She'd heard those words fall from his very perfect lips, and while she found him impossibly sexy, she also found him impossible. Men like Tate reminded her of her father.

That was the last type of man she wanted to be with. She'd witnessed her mother suffering through her crap marriage her whole life. Her entire family was in shambles, and it could all be traced back to her father.

A sobering thought, completely different from what her drunk mind was coming up with only moments before. So yeah. She didn't want a man like him. Not really. She didn't even want to fool around with a man who behaved like her father. That wasn't tempting at all.

Not one freaking bit.

TATE COULDN'T STOP sneaking glances at Wren, who was sitting so incredibly still with her eyes closed that he wondered if she was, um, alive?

But every few minutes she'd snore, a soft little snuffling sound that was kinda cute and reminded him that, yep, she was very much breathing. And willingly riding in his car so he could take her home. If it was any other woman, he'd be contemplating the many ways he could seduce her into his bed. How fast could he get her clothes off? How quick could he make her come? How long could he last once he was inside her? Because it had been a while since he'd been with someone, and this was Wren, after all. He'd quietly lusted after her for what felt like forever.

He had a hot woman who drove him crazy sitting in his car, and he couldn't do a damn thing about it. No way would he take advantage of her. She was buzzed. Not sloppy drunk, but still. She was sleeping, for the love of God.

Shaking his head, he blew out a harsh breath, forcing his concentration on the road and not the woman sitting in his passenger seat. But of course, he still kept stealing looks.

Pretty brown hair that looked soft to the touch. Long, thick eyelashes. Rosebud lips slightly parted. Creamy skin. Nice tits—come on, he was a man; he'd checked out her rack multiple times—and a nipped-in waist. Decent legs. She wasn't tall, so she didn't have those long, sexy legs like her good friend Delilah, but he couldn't complain. From what he remembered, she had a nice ass.

Great body, fiery attitude, smart mouth—what more could he ask for? He'd bet money she was wild in bed. Well. Maybe she wasn't wild in bed for anyone else, but he could probably help her unleash her inner vixen or whatever the hell women called it.

Tate frowned. Her inner vixen? He'd had a beer and a half if that, and he was thinking like a complete idiot. He blamed it on the woman. He blamed it on his lusty thoughts, which were doing him no favors since he couldn't act on shit. Not tonight, probably not ever, because he couldn't risk attempting *anything* with Wren Gallagher. She already bagged on him enough about his supposed man-whorish ways. She definitely had relationship material written all over her, and he didn't do that sort of thing. Ever.

She shifted in her seat, murmuring something unintelligible. He tilted his head toward her, trying to make out the words she said, but it sounded like a whole bunch of nothing.

Until he heard her drop *his* name amid all the other words he couldn't quite understand.

Tate frowned, clenching the steering wheel hard. No way did she just say his name in her sleep. He must've heard her wrong. Unless she was dreaming of kicking his ass—entirely possible—he doubted she thought of him ever. Certainly not while she was in dreamland.

But no. She said it again. Clear as day, followed by a sexy murmur that piqued his curiosity. Along with other parts of his body...

"What are you dreaming about over there?" he asked out loud, wanting to come out of his skin when she answered him.

"You."

He jerked the steering wheel to the right and hit the brakes, skidding across the road before he came to a full stop in front of someone's driveway. Studying her, he saw that her eyes were still closed, her body limp, a very satisfied smile curling her lush lips. She shifted in her seat, stretching her arms above her head, her smile growing, her eyes remaining closed. Her shoulders lifted, her breasts jiggling with the movement, and he practically had to shove his tongue back into his mouth, he was so mesmerized.

"Really?" he asked quietly as he shifted the vehicle into Park and turned so he was practically facing her. "Are you fucking with me, Gallagher?"

"Appropriate choice of words." She laughed, this throaty, sexy sound emanating from her like nothing he'd ever heard before. His cock strained against his fly and he reached down to adjust himself, wondering at Wren's transformation.

She's asleep, asshole. That explains her sudden transformation.

Yeah. He needed to remember that. She was sleeping. And probably dreaming—though it was interesting, the possibility of Wren dreaming about him. But how could he believe what she was telling him if she was half-asleep?

"Wren?" He actually said her real name instead of calling her Sparrow or Robin or whatever. He wasn't playing games any longer. But did he want her to wake up and realize her mistakes? Or keep sleeping and say things she wouldn't normally say when she was awake and lucid?

"Mmm-hmm?" She turned her head, her lids lifting to reveal those deep blue eyes. They looked hazy. She wasn't all there. He knew it.

Reaching out, he touched her cheek with just his fingertips. "You awake?"

"Oh, yeah." Her voice had this breathy quality that went straight to his dick. "I like it when you touch me."

Jeeeee-sus. He went completely still before he dropped his hand from her face. Man, he was in some serious trouble here if all she had to do was drop a few simple words and he was ready to tear her clothes off.

"Are we home yet?" She smiled and closed her eyes, snuggling her cheek against the seat. "I'm so tired. My head is spinning."

"Right. Let's get you home," he said, determination filling him as he put the car in gear and pulled back out onto the road.

He'd take her home, get her safely inside, and leave. Get out of there before he was tempted to do something epically stupid.

Like kiss her.

Chapter Three

A DEEP, RUMBLY voice sounded close to Wren's ear, encouraging her to wake up. But she didn't want to. It was nice, this dream she was having. In it, Tate was being really sweet and looking at her like he wanted to do something obscenely inappropriate to her. And she *wanted* him to do something obscenely inappropriate, especially if it involved taking their clothes off and lots of kissing and rubbing and touching.

That had to be the alcohol talking.

Her head was spinning. She was super tired and…oh my God, did Tate just scoop her up in his arms and haul her out of the car? Yes, he did. He was holding her close to his hard chest, his thick muscled arms banded around her as he turned away from the vehicle, the cool night air rushing over her skin and making her shiver. She wrapped her arms around his neck and clung to him, closing her eyes and pressing her face into his shoulder.

God, he smelled amazing, but that wasn't a revelation. The skin of his neck was hot. And so smooth. She wanted to kiss him right there, right at the spot where she could feel his pulse throb beneath her lips.

Yeah. The alcohol was still talking. Meaning she should absolutely not say one word until he was gone and she was alone. And even then she'd remain quiet because she'd be a straight-up wacko if she spent the rest of the night talking to herself about the man she was currently lusting after even though she shouldn't, right?

"Wren." He jiggled her in his arms, and she made a low murmuring sound, feigning sleep. Her lips brushed against his skin and he went completely still. "Wake up."

His voice was scratchy and strained, like she was pushing him close to the edge, but she kept her eyes tightly closed. Not wanting to see him. Not wanting him to see her. He readjusted his hold on her, clutching her even tighter, and a full-body shiver moved through her.

He felt it too. Of course, he did.

"Wren." A pause. He cleared his throat. "Baby." Another pause, his fingers tightening their grip on her. "Wake up."

Ooh, his saying her name in that dark-as-sin voice of his and then calling her *baby*? She may as well end up a melted puddle on the floor. "Mmm, what?" she asked irritably. Seriously, she *was* irritated. She wanted a few more moments to pretend that something would happen between them. It was better than the bitter disappointment she knew she'd experience once he was gone.

Wren cracked her eyes open, staring at his chest. Where did that thought come from?

"I need your keys," he said. "I can't open your front door without them."

"They're in the front pocket of my shorts." Let's see him try to grab those keys too. Any other time she'd bat his hands away and tell him to back off.

Not right now though.

"Swear to God, woman, you're trying to torture me," he muttered under his breath as he wrapped one arm tight around her and reached for the front of her shorts with his other hand. His fingers skimmed along her waist, shifting downward so he practically groped her crotch.

She squeezed her thighs together with a squeal, and he immediately jerked his hand away from her. "Sorry."

Wren said nothing, pressing her lips together when those sure fingers slipped into her front pocket and latched around her keys. It felt nice, him touching her.

Tate pressed the keys into her hand. "Unlock the door."

"But…"

"Do it, Raven." He stepped closer to her front door so it was in arm's reach.

Ooh. Back to the bird name-calling again. Growling under her breath, she thrust out her arm, the keys clutched in her fingers as she pushed the key into the lock, turning it with a vicious twist. Stupid man and his stupidly irritating jokes. All her earlier dreamy kissing thoughts evaporated as she struggled against his hold. She wanted out of his arms.

She wanted him out of here.

"Let me go," she demanded as he kicked the door open and strode inside her dark and tiny living room.

He set her down carefully and stepped away the moment her feet hit the floor, holding his hands up in front of him. "Guess you're awake now."

Tate was lucky she didn't knee him in the balls. Ugh. One minute she actually wanted to make out with him and the next she didn't even want him standing in the same room with her.

Which he was doing, by the way. Standing. In the same room with her. Filling it up with his arrogantly sexy presence, making her want to do something crazy.

Like jump him.

Nooooo. No, no, no. No jumping Tate Warren. Get him out of here. He makes you mad. He doesn't make you happy. Like…ever.

"I'm wide awake. I've also completely come to my senses." She tilted her chin up and narrowed her gaze, hoping she looked strong and capable. By the amusement she saw sparkling in his too-pretty eyes, she figured she looked silly instead. She still wouldn't back down though. "Thank you for the ride. You can go now."

He cocked a brow. "Don't you want me to tuck you in?"

No. No way did she want him to do that. What if he gave her a sweet, soft good-night kiss with those perfect lips of his, only for her to wrap her hand around his neck to keep him in place and pull him into her bed, and next thing they knew, they'd be tangled up in the sheets…

"I could sing you a song," he continued, just before he did indeed sing her a song. " 'Hush, little baby, don't say a word. Papa's gonna buy you a mockingbird.' " Tate started to laugh.

While her blood started to boil. "Get. Out." She bit the words out, tired of the mocking way he teased her. It wasn't funny anymore. None of it was.

No, more like it was frustrating. And confusing. Deep down inside, she knew she had a major, raging, out-of-control crush on Tate Warren.

And he considered her nothing but a joke.

"CAN I ASK you a personal question?" Tate tried his best to keep his tone nonchalant as he sat across from his friend and fellow employee West Gallagher. He didn't want to raise suspicion. He was back at work at the fire station, and it was a quiet afternoon. The engines were sitting in the garage, washed and polished, downright sparkling with cleanliness. The grounds were clean, as was the kitchen, and his crew was having siesta time. A nap was always necessary when they spent most of the previous night out on a medical aid call.

A single-vehicle accident had happened on the twisty highway that led into town. People drove too fast around those curves, especially out-of-towners. The car had rolled and slid down the embankment. They'd worked on the accident all night long.

Didn't matter how tired Tate was. He couldn't fall asleep. So he'd been scanning through his phone in the common area when West strolled in and sat on the couch across from him. A necessary distraction, considering Tate had too much on his mind. Well, someone in particular on his mind.

West's expression immediately turned wary. "Depends on what you're asking."

Hmm. How could he approach this topic when it was about West's little sister? The sister Tate currently couldn't stop thinking about? Ever since he'd left her at her cottage a few nights ago, she was all he thought about. How sweet and warm she'd felt in his arms. They way she'd murmured his name in his car while she was asleep. How angry she'd become when he sang that stupid lullaby.

How sexy she was when she was angry…

"It's no big deal." Tate shrugged. Smiled. Chuckled. "It's about Wren…"

West still glared at him. "Anything about my sister and you, forget it. You don't have my permission."

Tate's mouth popped open. What, like he needed his permission to mess around with Wren? Not that he'd ever tell West he wanted to "mess around" with his sister. "It's nothing like that."

"Come on. It's everything like that. You've got a thing for Wren, and she has a thing for you. The two of you have been circling each other like pissed-off cats ever since I rolled into town. God knows how long it's been going on before I got here." West leaned forward, intimidating as hell, but Tate refused to budge. He kept completely still. "I know what kind of guy you are."

Tate's brows rose. "Excuse me?"

"You're just like I was. And don't bother denying it either. You strut around town in your uniform trying to impress the ladies, and I'll give it to you. It works."

West's mouth thinned. "Doesn't seem to work on my sister though."

"Maybe I don't want it to work on your sister." He did not strut around town showing off. Well, not really.

"Please." West laughed. "You're definitely interested in Wren. But no way am I letting you near my baby sister. You're not worthy."

"What the fuck? How am I not worthy?" He really didn't want to have this conversation with West, but he'd brought it on himself, so he had no one else to blame. "Never mind. Don't tell me."

"Please. Allow me the *honor* of telling you." West leaned back in his chair, crossing his arms in front of his chest. "You're a player. I used to be one too. I know exactly what you do and what you're looking for. Commitment scares the shit out of you, and I get it. Trust me. But I'm not about to let you fuck around and fuck over my sister. That's the last thing I want for Wren." He at least had the decency to look uncomfortable.

"I don't want to hurt her," Tate mumbled, not willing to reveal much of anything else. Hell, he shouldn't have even said that. Hearing West's words, seeing the glower on his face, was the deterrent he needed. The reminder that even contemplating messing around with Wren was a big mistake.

Huge.

"If you mean that, then you'll leave her alone and let this be." West peered at him, his expression like stone. "I'm sure half the fun is the challenge."

"Kind of like Harper was a challenge for you?" Tate threw back at him.

Another big mistake. A muscle ticked in West's jaw. He looked pissed. Probably didn't like the fact that Tate mentioned his girl. And how rocky their relationship started.

"Don't bring Harper into this. You don't know her. You don't know what we have." West pointed a finger at him. "When it comes to my sister, you keep your hands off her. Understand?"

Tate nodded and leapt to his feet. He opened up an entire can of worms with this conversation. Now he was agreeing to whatever West demanded just to get him to shut up. "Understood."

Without another word he left the room and headed outside, taking a big, gulping breath of fresh air. Fucking Weston Gallagher was a little punk. Like he could tell him what to do. West could kiss his ass. If he wanted to see Wren, talk to her, hell, *fuck* her, he would.

And he wouldn't regret it. Neither would she. He'd make sure she was satisfied. He'd leave her with a smile.

That's what he was best at—leaving. He had that down pat.

Chapter Four

"WE'VE GOT A lead and we're fairly certain we know who's setting the fires," Josh Bailey said as he settled into the chair opposite Tate's desk.

Not a place Tate spent much time at, but since he'd been promoted to captain, he had to play at "man of authority" every once in a while. This afternoon was one of those times.

"You don't say?" Tate leaned back in his chair, waiting for the arson investigator to continue. The dude was all right. Most of the time he walked around like he had a stick up his ass and acted like he didn't trust anyone, but Tate understood. Coming into a small town as a stranger and trying to fit in was difficult.

Tate knew from firsthand experience. He'd been in Wildwood for only about a year, and pretty much everyone treated him like a stranger. It was even worse for Josh. He was investigating multiple arson fires that had been set over the last few months and had to question people. Josh was desperate to blend in and operate undercover, but everyone wondered who the new guy around town was.

"Yep." Josh nodded, his expression one of…excitement? That was the most emotion Tate had ever seen on the guy. He pretty much had one face at all times—serious. In other words, Josh gave Lane Gallagher a run for his money.

Of course, Lane was all smiles now that he was getting sex on a regular basis. Not that Tate could blame the guy. He'd be wearing a smile on his face too if he was getting some all the time.

Tate frowned. And why the hell wasn't he getting some exactly? There were plenty of summer girls who fit the bill. Gorgeous women on vacation looking for a quick fling. He'd indulged many times last year.

This summer was practically over, and he could hardly remember the last time he had sex. What the hell was wrong with him?

And why the hell hadn't Josh said anything else?

"Well, who is it then?" Tate asked.

Stony-faced Josh was back. "I can't tell you that."

"Then why even bring it up?"

"I just wanted you to know that hopefully we'll nail this guy and it'll be over soon." His lips went thin, his face downright expressionless. Tate felt like he was seeing all the faces of Josh in a matter of minutes. "We're going into full covert mode."

"Really?" Tate raised a brow. He'd heard enough undercover stories to know that Josh wasn't going to give him even a hint of information. He'd find out all of the details after the fact.

"Yeah. And that's all I can say about that." Josh stood and nodded once, in pure official mode. "I'm sure you'll hear if anything happens."

"Good luck," Tate called as Josh exited his office.

Weird. The guy runs in looking ready to burst with good news and then barely gives up any details? Why stop by in the first place?

Tate had a feeling Josh wasn't the best when it came to making friends. Tate, on the other hand, could make friends with anyone. That was why he had been promoted so quickly through the ranks at Cal Fire. Why he was so popular back in high school.

Why he was so good with the ladies.

Well, that and his face.

He could be an arrogant ass sometimes, but he wasn't stupid. He knew he was decent-looking. Combine that with his uniform, and forget it. The ladies swarmed every time he came around. Even old ladies went nuts over him. Whenever he went on a call at the local senior citizens' hall during bingo night—which was far too often—he always got his butt pinched by a gray-haired old woman. They cackled like mad when he whipped around to see who'd done it.

But how could he get mad? If they got a thrill by pinching his ass, then he wasn't going to complain. They were harmless.

Most of them, anyway.

Tate pushed away from the desk and stood, stretching his arms above his head. It had been quiet all day. He was off shift first thing tomorrow morning, and he couldn't wait. Planned to go straight home and collapse into bed. Hopefully he wouldn't dream of Wren either. He'd been having that problem lately, which wasn't good when he woke up with a tent in his pants—while on duty at the station.

Ah, Wren. He tried his best not to think about her during the day, but it proved difficult. Not that he'd put her out of his mind because of what West said yesterday. Hell no. He wasn't going to avoid her just because her asshole big brother told him to. West ordering him around only made him want to see her even more.

But he wouldn't.

He couldn't afford to think of her. She was too much of a distraction, and he needed to focus. He had a job to do—he was responsible for his crew, responsible for the entire station and even the whole damn town of Wildwood. They had an arsonist on their hands, and whoever their firebug was, the guy was on a serious tear. The most recent fire that started on Ridge Point Road had burned thousands of acres and threatened the town before they were finally able to first control and then contain it.

But that had been over a week ago. All had been quiet since, which made Tate feel uneasy. Their local firebug liked to disappear for a bit, lulling everyone into a sense of calm before he went back at it.

Or she. Their arsonist could be a woman too. Hell, he remembered hearing about a case a few years ago where a married couple tried to burn down their entire community. Once the trial was all said and done, they both got seventy years in prison.

Tate shook his head. People were strange.

He exited the tiny office and headed outside, stopping short when he found West standing mere feet away, his arms wrapped around Harper and their lips locked.

Shuffling his feet, Tate coughed discreetly, but they still didn't come up for air. He cleared his throat.

Nothing.

Hell. "Uh, you two should think about getting a room," Tate called.

Harper immediately broke the kiss and shoved West away, her entire face red as she turned to Tate. "Um, hey." She waved, unable to meet his gaze.

He wanted to laugh but figured he'd piss West off, so he remained quiet. West glared but stepped away from Harper, smoothing his hands down the front of his uniform shirt. "What's up?" He gave the universal man chin lift at Tate.

"I should go," Harper said as she stood on tiptoe to kiss West's cheek. She patted his chest, smiled at Tate, and hurried away in a flurry of motion, her flip-flops slapping against the sidewalk as she headed toward the parking lot.

"Did she bring a pie?" he asked once Harper was gone.

Harper stopped by the station when she could, always with a sweet, shy smile for West and sometimes bearing pie from the Bigfoot Diner, the restaurant her grandma owned. Her grandma was famous for her desserts, especially her pies. If Tate was dating Harper, he'd be as big as a house and happy as fuck from eating all the pie he could ever want.

"No, she didn't bring a pie." West rubbed his hand over his head, sending Tate a pointed look. "I forgot my wallet at home when I came into work yesterday and she finally brought it by."

"Ah." Sounded like an excuse to Tate but whatever. Who was he to judge?

"She also said she wanted to have you over for dinner Saturday, if we don't end up having to work."

"I'd love to. Can I make a request for dessert?" Tate grinned, and West gave him the finger, chuckling under his breath as he turned and walked away.

Tate whistled as he walked toward the garage. He knew West was still bent out of shape about the Wren thing, but he'd get over it.

Eventually.

"WHO ALL IS coming to this dinner?" Wren asked Delilah as she applied black liquid eyeliner on her upper lids. She loved eyeliner pens. They made the cat-eye technique so much easier.

"Me and Lane. West and Harper, of course. And…" Delilah's voice drifted until she became silent.

Wren stared at her iPhone where it sat on the bathroom counter, willing her friend to finish her sentence. It was Saturday night, she was getting ready to go over to her friends' house for dinner, and she had Delilah on speaker while she finished putting on her makeup. "And who else?" she asked sharply when Delilah didn't say anything.

"Fine, it's Tate. But don't make a big deal about it. Harper's not trying to set you two up or anything. She was feeling bad because, or so she claims, he's alone all the time, and she wanted to include him in our group stuff," Delilah explained.

"Oh, come on. Tate Warren is not lonely. He's always got girls falling at his feet." Wren leaned closer to the mirror. Her hand was too shaky as she tried to draw the eyeliner along her lash line, so she set the pen on the counter. Why were her hands shaking? It had nothing to do with Tate, did it?

She hadn't seen him since he dropped her off at her place five days ago. After he claimed he wanted to tuck her into bed and she'd been so tempted to let him. Until he sang that stupid, *stupid* song and pissed her off.

The next morning she woke up with a raging headache and massive regret. Regret that she ever thought something could happen between her and Tate. She realized her mistake—drinking around Tate got her into trouble. Alcohol made her lose her inhibitions. She'd been so tempted to make a move on him, and she was sort of glad that she didn't.

She was also sort of sad that she didn't. Not that she'd ever admit that out loud.

"Not really. Tate's been working too much this summer. No way he had time to go out with anyone," Delilah said, interrupting Wren's thoughts. "He might flirt or whatever, but that's how he puts the women he deals with at ease."

Uh-huh. That sounded like an excuse.

"Besides, this is all coming from Harper," Delilah continued. "She's a total mama bear, you know. Always wanting to take care of people—bring them into the fold and make sure they're happy."

"I think he's perfectly capable of taking care of himself," Wren retorted, taking a step back so she could check herself out more fully in the mirror. Did she look all right? Her hair was kind of limp, but it had been so hot today she'd put it in a ponytail. That's why she wore a strapless sundress that was a long column of cobalt blue. Nothing too sexy. It wasn't like she had huge boobs, and the dress covered her to her toes.

But her shoulders were exposed and she had the slightest hint of cleavage going on. Would Tate like it? Or would he think she was trying too hard?

Wren frowned. When did she care what Tate thought? And why did he always pop into her head at the strangest times? She wasn't supposed to like him. After all, she was the one who always instigated their arguments. Though someone had once called their arguing foreplay—probably Delilah—and, well, maybe it was.

Oh God. Maybe it *was.*

"Well, it doesn't really matter if he can take care of himself or not because he'll be there tonight. I thought I should prepare you, considering the simmering—yet somehow sexual—hostility that's always brewing between you two," Delilah said.

Wren dug through the narrow drawer she kept all of her cosmetics in. It was a mess, and all she wanted to find was her mascara. "What do you mean, sexual hostility?"

"You two act the same way whenever you're together. You make a snide remark, he flirts, you roll your eyes, he smiles—and seriously, Wren, when Tate smiles, it's devastatingly cute—then you say something rude, he implies that he wants to see you naked, you walk away in an irritated huff, and he sneaks looks at you whenever you're not paying attention."

Wren went completely still, gripping the edge of the counter. Was Delilah for real? Is that what they did every single time? And he snuck looks at her? She had no idea. "We're not that bad," she protested, her voice weak.

"You so are," Delilah said firmly. "I think you two are hot for each other, but you just don't want to admit it."

"I'm not hot for him." It was an automatic response, denying her attraction to Tate.

Oh God. Was she really attracted to *Tate*? Or was she crazy?

"Well, I think he's hot for you. And it's silly how you keep him at arm's length." Delilah's voice lowered, like she didn't want Lane to hear her, which was probably the case. "He's gorgeous, Wren. Like drop-dead, ridiculously good-looking. You should go for it."

"He's not my type."

"He's *everyone's* type. Smart, funny, beyond handsome, and he has a good job. He's a total catch."

"Well, I don't want him. I'd throw that catch right back into the ocean." Wren winced. She sounded stupid. Typical. Tate rendered her stupid. She didn't want to talk about him anymore. She'd say something even dumber, and Delilah would totally call her on it. "Let's change the subject."

"You're making lame-ass remarks and want to change the subject. I think that means you're hot for him."

Freaking Delilah.

"Stop trying to make a match. It's not working." Damn it, it was so working. Delilah was right. Tate was totally her type. Well, not really, but it didn't matter. She would never toss him into the ocean. She'd rather toss him into her bed.

Ugh. No. Bad idea. Epically awful, terrible idea.

"Please. I think it would totally work. You two would be so cute together."

"He's too good-looking." Wren stared down at her phone, surprised she was about to admit one of her many insecurities when it came to Tate Warren. "I don't date men who are better-looking than me."

"Are you serious right now? Babe, you're beautiful. Have you seen the way he looks at you?"

"How does he look at me?" Wren asked, her voice small. She nibbled on her thumbnail, scared to hear what Delilah had to say.

"Like he wants you. Like you amuse and intrigue him, all at once. Are you wearing your hair up?"

Delilah's abrupt change of subject threw her for a second. "Um, yeah?" She turned her head, looking at her reflection. Her high ponytail looked good—if she did say so herself—and it worked double duty considering how hellaciously hot it was outside.

"Take it down. Now," Delilah demanded.

"Yes, Mom." Wren pulled the hair tie out, her stick-straight hair falling down past her shoulders.

"Wear your hair down, slick on some shiny lip gloss, and make sure to do that cat-eye thing you're so good at.

You'll slay him dead. See you soon." Delilah made kissy noises, and then she was gone.

Wren scowled at herself in the mirror, then snatched the eyeliner pen from the counter. She shouldn't want to dress up for him. She wasn't going to dinner tonight to impress a man. That was silly.

But she took a deep breath, told herself to calm down, and started to reapply the eyeliner, telling herself to take her time and get it right. She wanted to look good. Not for Tate.

But for herself.

Chapter Five

TATE HAD A plan—and that plan was to ignore Wren as much as possible tonight. He needed to stay away from her in order to keep his sanity. She had a way of getting under his skin just by looking at him, not to mention when she talked to him. Hearing her voice, seeing her expressive face, just being in her presence made him feel alive.

But he'd pissed her off the last time they were together, and he figured it best to keep his distance. No matter how difficult that might be.

He'd been to a few of Harper and West's get-togethers over the summer and they were always crowded. Full of people and music and food and plenty of beer flowing. They definitely knew how to throw a party. He arrived at West and Harper's place and didn't see Wren's car in the parking lot. He figured he would have the upper hand when she finally appeared, already comfortable and chatting someone up, preferably a pretty girl. If the party was a real rager, he might never encounter Wren at all.

But once he walked through the door, he realized quickly that it wasn't a typical party. Oh, Harper pretended that it was, but really? It was a couples thing. A couples-only dinner thing.

Meaning he was paired up with Wren for the evening. *Shit.*

His friends said nothing, the pussy-whipped fuckers. He nursed a beer and bit his tongue, afraid he might say something rude to Harper since she was the one who'd put him in this position.

Wren was going to kill him when she discovered what their so-called friends had done.

When she finally walked through the front door, he sent her a helpless look, one that he hoped said, *I had nothing to do with this. Don't hate me.*

He swore he could see the momentary panic on her face when her gaze swept the room, noting how many people weren't there. She sent a death stare Harper's way before she started her approach.

Toward him.

Tate tried not to act like an asshole and gape at her, but it proved difficult considering how damn beautiful she looked. She wore a strapless blue dress that covered even her feet but didn't really show off any of the curves he knew she had. That was only a minor disappointment since her shoulders and arms were bare, revealing her collarbones and the very, very top of her breasts. She didn't have it all hanging out—what a shame—but there was the slightest hint of cleavage, and she kept yanking the top up self-consciously.

Weirdo that he was, he liked the glimmer of self-consciousness, considering she made him a little nervous when pretty much nothing made him feel that way. He wondered if he made her nervous too.

Damn. He couldn't stop staring at her. He'd bet big money her skin was soft. And he'd bet she smelled extra good tonight too.

She stopped just in front of him, and he snapped his lips shut, trying to appear unaffected.

"Tate." Her voice was icy.

He started to sweat. "Dove. Though I should probably call you Bluebird, what with the dress."

Her gaze narrowed. She looked pissed. What else was new? Didn't she see he teased no one else like he teased her? It was a sign of affection, damn it. He *liked* her.

Okay, fine. He more than liked her.

He wanted to see her naked. Have sex. Fuck her. Make her come. Slip his dick in her mouth. Feel her fingers curl around his dick. Whatever it took, whatever she was up for, that's what he wanted.

She sighed, the sound full of irritation. "So typical."

"What's that supposed to mean?" He frowned.

"You go for the obvious every single time. Calling me bird names. It's becoming old news."

He reached over and tugged on a glossy strand of brown hair, his gaze locking with hers. "You don't like the bird names?" He liked her hair down. Could imagine gathering it into his hand and pulling as he fucked her from behind.

"I hate the bird names."

"Why? It's fun."

"Maybe to you." She lifted her chin. "I find them annoying."

"I hate to break it to you, but…" He paused, taking a step closer until his mouth was by her ear. "You think pretty much everything I do is annoying."

She was quiet for a moment and he didn't move, her ear so temptingly close he wanted to lick it. Nibble it. Whisper dirty things in it.

"True," she finally said on a shuddery exhale. She took a step back, as if needing the distance. "I guess you just can't help yourself."

"I guess not. I'm just teasing you, Wren. I don't mean to irritate you." He decided to change the subject before she ran with this and continued to insult him. "You think they're trying to pair us together?"

Her eyes went almost comically wide, and she rested a hand on her chest, covering her cleavage. A damn shame if anyone asked him. "Noooo. You don't really think so, do you?" She was most definitely mocking him.

But he chose to ignore the mocking tone. "Shouldn't we just make them happy?"

Those pretty blues went from wide to narrowed in a few seconds flat. "So you want to try out being a couple just to make them happy?"

"I have a feeling I could make you pretty happy too, if you know what I mean." He smiled. She frowned. But he caught a flicker of something in her eyes, something that looked suspiciously like…interest.

But any hint of interest was gone in an instant. "You're incredibly arrogant."

He shrugged, said nothing. But deep inside his heart thundered, and nerves ate at his gut. This girl set him on edge. He told himself to stay away, yet here he was, like he couldn't help himself.

Which he sort of couldn't.

Besides, their friends actually wanted them together—at least, the women did. It was obvious. He was on board with the idea—as long as she didn't expect anything serious.

Not that Wren seemed to expect much of anything when it came to him. She flat out didn't like him. He didn't get it. Could it be brotherly influence? He thought he was friends with both Lane and West, but maybe they hated the idea of him dating their baby sister.

"I'm still mad at you, you know." Her sweet voice broke through his thoughts, and he turned to look at her.

"For what?" he asked, taking a swig from his beer. He was always pissing this girl off, so what else was new?

"For the mockingbird bit. When you sang me the lullaby." She crossed her arms in front of her chest, plumping up her breasts, and his gaze dropped as if he had no control. When it came to Wren, he was learning that was pretty much the truth. And damn, she was really giving him an eyeful. "You blew your chance."

Tate wondered if she'd blow him. Hell, he wondered if she'd be up for him sliding his cock between her perfect tits. Had she ever let a guy do that to her before?

Something stirred in his belly at the possibility, and he shoved it away. Jealousy had no place here.

None.

"Eyes up here, jackass," she muttered, and he jerked his gaze from her chest to find her watching him with a scowl. "Did you even hear what I said?"

He was about to take another drink and he paused, lowering his beer. Yeah, he'd heard her. "Blew what chance?" he asked carefully.

"You know exactly what I'm talking about." It was her turn to lean in close to him. She dropped her arms, her right breast rubbing against his chest, and he wondered if she did that on purpose. "I was a little drunk that night. And to be honest, I was also perfectly willing. Right until you sang the stupid song."

Perfectly willing. Perfectly willing. Those two simple words were on repeat in his head. Perfectly willing for what? Anything? Everything?

She must've seen the questioning in his eyes, because she smiled smugly, her delicate eyebrows rising. "Yes. *Whatever* you were up for, I would've done. But now you'll never know, right? You seriously blew it."

And with that, she turned and walked away.

WREN WAS SHAKING, her stomach twisting into knots as she made her way across the room, never once looking back to see if Tate was watching.

But she could feel his eyes on her and knew without a doubt that he was most definitely watching her. She made sure she put some extra sway in her step, hoping like crazy that her words had filled him with total regret.

She was still mad about that night. That he sang that stupid song and ruined her mood. For the way he made fun of her yet somehow made her feel sexy, all at the same time.

His gaze had been appreciative when he looked at her, and he'd straight up ogled her chest just now. She acted like she hated it, but really?

Damn it, she'd freaking loved it. She couldn't remember the last time a man had looked at her like Tate just did. Her skin had grown warm and her nipples hard beneath the dress. She wore no bra, so she could only hope he hadn't noticed.

But knowing Tate Warren? He totally noticed.

"What did you just say to him?" Harper asked when Wren stopped to stand by her side. "He looks like he just swallowed his tongue."

"Nothing much." Wren shrugged. She couldn't tell Harper what she said. It was bad enough how hard their friends were pushing them on each other. "I can't believe you did this, by the way."

The innocent look on Harper's face was a bit much. "What are you talking about?"

"Give me a break. You're trying to put the two of us together. Your couples-only dinner party is a dead giveaway."

"I don't like that we're all coupled up and you're not." Harper frowned. "I don't want you lonely."

Oh God. She really didn't want Harper and everyone else feeling sorry for her. Talk about pitiful. "I'm not lonely. I work too much to ever be lonely." Sort of a lie, sort of the truth.

"The fact that you think working too much is totally okay *totally* isn't." Harper sent her a stern look. "I think you two would make a perfect couple."

"I can't stand him." *Lies.* "He makes me insane." *Truth.* "He's always making fun of me." *And I sort of love it.*

"He's just teasing."

"Yeah, well, sometimes it hurts." *Not really.*

Okay, yes really. But only when I believe he sees me only as a joke. That's when it hurts.

Growing up, her brothers never took her seriously. And her father definitely never took her seriously. Even her mom—whom she adored and would do anything for—didn't believe she could do much beyond marry well and raise a family. Those had been her mom's goals, so she believed they should be Wren's too. Maybe she had ambitions. Goals. Maybe they had nothing to do with this town or the work she was doing. Maybe she needed to leave.

But where would she go? Why did she constantly beat herself up for staying in Wildwood? Harper left and came back. Delilah was perfectly content.

So why did she feel so restless?

"Should I have West talk to him?" Harper offered, breaking into Wren's wayward thoughts.

"God, no. Keep my brother out of it." Wren shook her head, sending a worried glance in West's direction. He was talking to Tate, but they seemed friendly enough. Tate was even smiling and laughing, so that had to be a good sign.

The last thing she wanted was one or all of her brothers running to her defense. It was fine in school, not so much in adulthood.

Besides, she didn't want to scare Tate away. Not when she was finally starting to realize she liked him.

"He seems into you." At Wren's frown Harper continued. "Tate. I think he likes you."

"He wants to sleep with me." Harper beamed, and Wren almost hated to be the one to shut her down. "But there's a big difference between wanting to sleep with me and actually *liking* me, Harper. You know this."

"So it's just a sex thing?" Harper sounded disappointed.

"I don't think Tate knows how to commit. And I refuse to get involved with a man who can't commit." She tried to act tough, like she wasn't bothered by her friends finding love, but she yearned for the same thing. She wanted to find a man who wanted to be with her, who loved only her.

Considering their less-than-perfect upbringing and the example their parents had set, Wren was surprised by the devotion her brothers displayed toward their women—all three of them. The youngest, Holden, had been in the longest relationship of them all, and he was still madly in love with his girlfriend, Kirsten. West and Lane followed Harper and Delilah around like lovesick puppy dogs.

Wren wanted that. She wanted a strong man who was confident, who knew what he wanted and went after it. And once he got it, he worked his hardest to keep it. She'd had a boyfriend long ago who she'd believed was the one.

Her old high school love, the boy she gave her virginity to. She'd been the devoted one in that relationship. Following Levi around like he was the man of her dreams, secretly planning their future wedding, writing her name in the back of her school notebooks with his last name attached to hers.

Levi Hamilton

Wren Gallagher Hamilton

Wren Hamilton

Levi and Wren Hamilton

Mrs. Wren Hamilton

Yeah, she'd truly believed they were the perfect couple...until they weren't anymore.

And though she hated to admit it, she'd never really gotten over the way he dumped her. Out of nowhere, just before he left for college. She was a year younger and had been fully prepared for their upcoming long-distance relationship. Couldn't deny the little thrill that buzzed through her every time she thought about having a boyfriend in *college*.

But he'd broken up with her the day before he left, explaining that she deserved her freedom and so did he. During their time apart, he knew they would change too much. He couldn't stand the thought of her sitting at home waiting for him, missing him, when she should be truly experiencing her senior year and having fun.

She'd cried, she'd become unbelievably angry, and then she'd decided to have way too much fun just to prove to Levi that she could. She'd ended up getting in trouble. Doing bad in school, skipping classes, falling in with the wrong crowd. She'd grown distant with Harper and Delilah. They were older than her and already graduated from high school, so it was natural. She'd forcefully distanced herself from everyone.

It had been a brief moment in time when she had pushed all her limits and done stupid things, just to prove that she could. And it scared her, everyone's reaction to her wild behavior. Her parents blustered and threatened. Her brothers drove her crazy with their increasingly overprotective behavior. The real kicker? When her father told her she'd amount to absolutely nothing.

That had hurt. More than she ever admitted. Not that she told anyone he said that.

Now she pushed no limits. She played it safe.

Always.

"I think a just-sex thing would be ideal if you asked me," Harper said, knocking Wren from her thoughts.

Wren gaped at her friend. "Are you for real right now?"

Harper shrugged, glancing around to make sure no one heard her before she explained. "You were in a serious relationship when you were basically a kid. You went wild for a little bit, and then you calmed down. You haven't really done much since. Having casual sex with a gorgeous man would be a surefire way to cure your blues."

"Who said I had the blues?"

Harper met her gaze, her expression serious. "Are you really happy here, Wren? I feel like most of the time you're just waiting for something to happen to you. Like you're this close to running out of town and never looking back."

She'd never told anyone she wanted out of here. She was sort of ashamed for feeling that way. Look what happened when West bailed for all those years. They were all angry with him, including her. Her family would be so mad if she left, especially after everything that happened with their mom's health. She was okay, but Wren was the one who helped her. Drove her to doctor's appointments, made sure she picked up her meds, followed up to make sure she was actually taking those meds...

There were responsibilities she couldn't abandon, no matter how much she might secretly want to.

"This is my home," Wren said, her voice sincere. "I would never leave Wildwood."

"You're allowed to leave if you want. I know you have ties here. Your family, your friends, your investment in the dance studio." Harper reached out and touched her arm. "But you can do whatever you want. No one is stopping you. Heck, you're also allowed to indulge in hot casual sex with a very hot man. You're an adult, Wren. You can do whatever you want—even Tate."

Wren laughed and shook her head. "Thanks for giving me permission, but I think I'm going to pass. I'm perfectly content with my life, despite what you think."

But she couldn't shake what Harper said. It stuck with her the rest of the night, reminding her that maybe she *wasn't* content with her lot in life. She was in her mid-twenties, and she didn't have a serious boyfriend. Didn't even have a boy toy, and yeah, there was something incredibly wrong with that.

Not that it was all about sex and finding her identity with a man. No, she'd proved she could be successful on her own. Could she leave though? Maybe she could find a job in a bigger city. A position with great benefits and the potential for advancement. She'd had big dreams as a kid, many of them involving leaving this small town for the bright lights of the big city. So cliché, but back when she was a teen it was also so true.

She'd just never had the guts to do it. Knew what it felt like to be second choice—forgotten by both her boyfriend and her brothers. She didn't want anyone to feel like they were unimportant, that she wouldn't put them first, so she'd stayed.

Even if it meant hurting herself.

"You okay there, Woodpecker?"

They'd just sat down to dinner—surprise, Tate was sitting next to her—and of course, he had to go and say something annoying.

Wren offered him a polite smile that felt more like a bearing of teeth. "Shouldn't you be the one called Woodpecker, considering I don't have one?"

He chuckled, the low, warm sound stirring something deep within her. "I'm surprised you didn't call me a pecker."

"You're the one who said it first," she said sweetly as she reached for her water glass. The table was fully set, and Harper had used her grandma's china and finest silverware. Even the good crystal was out, with water and wineglasses at every setting. Harper really outdid herself.

Wren wondered at the formality of it. This dinner party was a serious affair compared with the barbecue and keg gatherings they normally had. Was something important happening? This had to be about more than just setting her up with Tate Warren, right?

Harper brought out a salad course first, setting the plates in front of everyone as she moved quickly around the table, falling into her chair when she finished. "Dig in!"

Tate stared at the array of silverware spread out on each side of his plate. "I'm afraid I'll use the wrong fork," he explained when he caught Wren watching him.

"Outside in," she told him, earning a frown for her efforts. "Start with the outside fork and keep working in."

"Ah, thanks." He picked up the salad fork and smiled at her, the sight of it frazzling a few of her brain cells. He was too handsome for his own good, and that smile… "I'm not much for formal dining."

"Me either," she said, leaning into him so her shoulder brushed his. He turned his head toward her, his smile soft, his green gaze roaming all over her face.

"Better at it than I am," he said. "Guess I'll need to keep you by my side tonight."

For once, she had no snarky retort, no smartass reply. She just stared at him, wondering at her quiet reaction, at the way her heart raced when she saw the hungry glow in his eyes.

Worried she might like it—like Tate—far too much.

THERE WAS A salad course. A soup course came next—both the salad and soup were delicious, as were the homemade rolls prepared by Harper's grandma—so when the main course finally rolled around, Tate was pretty full of food and beer.

Oh, and Wren. Beautiful, nonsnarky, teaching-him-how-to-be-a-classy-dude Wren. She instructed him on which piece of silverware to use next, whether he should pass to the left or right, and how much butter he should slather on the warm roll he'd attempted to slice open with a knife.

That was a no go, according to Wren. "Rip it open with your hands," she instructed him, demonstrating with her own roll.

He'd like to rip something open with his hands—like her dress. Or hey, her panties would be fun to rip open. Would she ever let him try something like that?

Probably not, so he'd have to settle for the fantasy instead.

There were little candles on the table and the overhead chandelier was dimmed low. The light was mellow, as was the mood. All Tate could hear was the clink of silverware on very thin, white plates with little pink roses dotting the edges.

This fancy dinner had nothing to do with the potential pairing of him and Wren.

And no one was asking what was up either. Delilah and Lane spent most of the meal making lovey eyes at each other. To the point where Tate did his damnedest not to look in their direction for fear of feeling like he was spying on an intimate moment. Harper was the harried hostess, and Tate could tell it was driving West crazy.

Then there was Wren. Bluebird. Dove. She was fairly quiet, which he found unusual. There was a nervous edge to the air, one he couldn't quite put his finger on, but it was there. Hovering in the room, making everyone cast wary glances at each other.

It was in between dinner and dessert, after the plates had been cleared and Harper was offering coffee to accompany the dessert, when West stood, grabbed hold of her hand, and demanded that she sit down.

"But I need to get the dessert," she protested, looking flustered.

"Sit down, woman," West commanded, and she did, her eyes wide as he knelt onto one knee in front of her.

"Oh my God," Wren whispered, glancing over her shoulder to look at Tate. "What is he doing?" she squeaked.

Tate shrugged, though he had a feeling he knew exactly what was happening.

"It's like you knew I had this planned so you put together an extra special dinner just for the occasion." West grabbed hold of Harper's hand and held it loosely in his own. "Baby, I love you."

"I love you too." She glanced around the room, her nervous gaze skipping over every one of them. "But you're holding up dessert."

"Dessert can wait. I need to ask you a question first." West reached into the front pocket of his jeans, pulling out a ring with a giant, flashing diamond. "I know we've only been together for a short time, but I've known you all my life. I feel like I've loved you most of my life too. I don't want to wait a proper amount of time—when I know, I know. And Harper, I know I want you to be my wife. Will you marry me?"

Tears sprang to Harper's eyes as she murmured her answer just before she lunged for West, wrapping her arms around his neck as their mouths met in a sweet kiss.

"Don't leave us hanging! What did she say?" Delilah asked, breaking the silence in the room.

West and Harper pulled away from each other, Harper's arms still around his neck. "She said yes," he said.

Everyone started talking at once, Delilah clapping as she practically bounced out of her chair. Lane went to his brother, who stood with Harper clutched close to his side, and enveloped them both into a hug. West mentioned champagne, and Delilah went to get it from the kitchen.

Wren never said a word. She remained completely still in her chair, her hands clutching the edge of the table, her head bent, as if she was staring at something particularly fascinating. Tate wanted to say something to her, ask her if she was all right, but what if she wasn't? What would he do then?

Instead he stood and went to West and Harper, offering his friend a congratulatory handshake and embracing Harper until West told him to let go of his fiancée. Which made Harper dissolve into near hysterical giggles, and they hadn't even popped open the champagne yet.

The night had taken a weird but happy turn.

Wren finally pushed her chair away from the table and approached the newly engaged happy couple, the tremulous smile curling her lips making Tate nervous. She hugged both West and Harper, quietly told them both she was so happy for them. She lingered in the room, her smile strained, her eyes sad. He wanted to go to her, wanted to say something, offer her comfort, whatever he could. But she'd probably just turn him away.

"Champagne time!" Delilah burst out of the kitchen carrying a bottle in one hand and some glasses in the other. "Who's ready to toast West and Harper?"

As they all rushed toward Delilah to grab a glass, Tate glanced around the room in search of Wren, but she was nowhere to be found. Concerned, he took off down the hall and stopped in front of the bathroom, rapping on the closed door three times, but there was no response.

He pressed his ear against the door, listening for a sign of life. Anything to indicate Wren was in there.

But he heard nothing.

"Wren." He grabbed hold of the doorknob and gave it a shake, but it was locked. "You all right?"

"Can't a girl pee in peace?" she wailed from within the bathroom.

He paused in his rattling the doorknob, feeling like a jackass. "Sorry. I'll leave you al—"

The door swung open, Wren standing before him, her eyes watery, tears streaking down her cheeks. She reached for him, taking his hand and yanking him into the bathroom before she slammed the door and turned the lock back into place.

"Don't leave," she murmured, reminding him of the night in the bar, when she'd looked so sad and a little drunk, grabbing hold of him and basically begging him not to go.

She was doing it again, only this time she was desperately trying to hold it together and having a hell of a time. He didn't like it. At all. Helpless crying chicks weren't his scene, and he glanced over his shoulder at the closed door, wondering how the hell he could get out of this and not piss her off or upset her more.

"Don't ask if I'm all right." Her voice was shaky, and she ran her index fingers beneath her eyes at the same time, catching a few tears and smeared mascara. "I'm fine. I promise."

Wren didn't look fine—emotionally fine, that was. Oh, she was fine as hell in that pretty dress with those bare shoulders and that cleavage, but otherwise, she seemed a little unstable.

Not that he was going to point that out.

Was she drunk? She'd had at least one glass of wine at dinner, but maybe she had more than he realized.

"It just happened so fast, you know? They've only been seeing each other for a few months and now they're getting married. I'm happy for them, I swear. It's just...I..." She pressed her lips together as if she needed to contain a sob and closed her eyes, shaking her head with a sniff.

Tate felt the panic rising within him. He didn't know what to do, what to say, how to comfort her. So he just remained quiet and let her talk, let her get it out.

"Everyone's paired off, you know? They're doing something with their lives, they have someone they love, and they're moving forward. While I'm still here, stuck. Though I shouldn't make this about me." She leaned against the counter and tilted her head back, staring up at the ceiling. "I'm acting incredibly selfish, running off to cry like a baby in the bathroom. I should be out there toasting them and talking bridesmaid dresses with Delilah."

"You don't have to if you don't want to." He moved toward her, nearly stepping on the hem of her dress. The bathroom was tiny, and he felt like he could hardly move without accidentally touching her. Not that touching Wren was ever an accident. "They'll understand."

"No, they won't." She looked at him, her smile weak, her entire demeanor so incredibly vulnerable he was tempted to wrap her up in his arms and never let her go. "Let me wash my face and then we'll go back out."

Tate frowned. "You want me to go first?" The others might think they were up to no good, alone in the bathroom.

She shook her head. "Hold my hand when we walk out there. Let's give them the show they want, okay?"

No way was he going to protest. "Whatever you want, Dove." Whatever made her happy.

For once, she didn't protest or give him shit about the bird name. "Why are you being so nice to me?"

"Because I like you." Reaching out, he touched her cheek with the back of his fingers. Her eyes slid closed, and she sighed, the sound so full of longing it touched something deep within him. Something he wanted to explore further.

With Wren.

She said nothing in reply. Just turned on the sink and splashed water on her cheeks, before wiping them with a hand towel. When she faced him, she squared her shoulders, trying her best to put on a brave front. "Let's go."

He unlocked the door, took her hand, and they exited the bathroom.

Together.

WREN WAS A bitch, a terrible friend and sister who couldn't support the people she loved during a time when they needed her the most. She'd run and hid in the bathroom like a jealous woman, crying into her hands, letting the guilt eat at her as she tried her best to fight against her confused emotions.

She really hoped her face wasn't too red from the pitiful crying. She'd mentally told herself to get over it. But get over...what exactly? She was thrilled West just asked Harper to marry him. One of her best friends would now be a member of her family. Life couldn't get any better than that.

So why the earlier tears? Why the brief moment of crushing disappointment? It wasn't directed at her brother and her friend. More like it was directed at...herself. Silly, she knew this. She had no boyfriend, not even a real serious prospect, and besides, she didn't need a man to make her life complete.

But seeing all the love between West and Harper. Watching her friend try her best to make the dinner as special as possible and her brother busting out a gorgeous ring while on one knee. It was all so incredibly romantic that it made Wren's heart swell...

And then bust wide open.

That Tate was the one who ran to her rescue wasn't lost on her. That he didn't give her shit or tell her to get it together helped tremendously. He said nothing, just watched her as she tried to compose herself and explain herself, all at once. But he never demanded an explanation.

He just wanted to be there for her. Period.

Even when he called her Dove, she couldn't complain. It was sweet the way he said it, his voice soft, his gaze warm. He'd taken her hand and led her back out to the tiny dining room, tugging her toward her friends, who embraced her all at once, Delilah and Harper hugging her so hard they almost toppled over.

"Are you okay?" Harper asked close to her ear.

Nodding, Wren pulled away from them, offering up a shaky smile. Damn it, she really needed to get her emotions in check. "I'm happy for you. Seriously."

"But—" Harper started to protest, and Wren cut her off.

"No *buts*. I can't believe it happened this fast, but asking you to marry him is the best thing West could've ever done for himself. For all of us. You two are perfect for each other." Wren's smile grew. "You're going to be my sister now."

"I know!" Harper squealed, pulling her in for a hug again. "I can't wait."

Wren couldn't wait either.

West pushed a glass of champagne into her hand and made a toast, thanking all of them for being here tonight.

"I wouldn't have it any other way," he said solemnly as he lifted his glass into the air, his gaze only for Harper. "To my future bride, for making me the happiest man on earth tonight."

Someone else said cheers, and then they were all clinking glasses and drinking, Wren swallowing every drop of her champagne in one giant gulp.

Liquid courage was definitely on the agenda again tonight.

Once the gushy toasts were out of the way—during which Wren might've drank three full glasses—music was turned on, so loud it drowned out her thoughts, her worries, her troubles. She helped clean the kitchen for a little bit before Harper shooed her away. She went outside to the backyard, another full glass of champagne dangling from her fingers, moving in time to the beat of the song that was playing.

Wren wasn't much on dancing. That was more Delilah's scene. Though with enough champagne in her, she found herself swaying to the beat, her eyes sliding closed. The bass throbbed, and the alcohol flowing through her veins was just enough to make her feel loose.

Free.

Her eyes popped open to find Tate standing a few feet away, clutching a bottle of water and watching her with an amused expression on his face.

"Am I entertaining you?" she asked, raising a brow. "Want me to put on a little show?"

"You're always entertaining, Dove." He smirked. "And please, don't stop dancing on my part."

There was no one else around them, so she felt bold. Like she could say anything. "I could do a striptease." Wren executed a little drunken twirl, her glass slipping from her fingers as she nearly fell, tripping over the too-long skirt of her dress. Tate lunged forward and caught her before she hit the ground, gathering her in his arms and holding her close to his chest.

His very firm, very warm chest.

Breathless, she gazed up at him, noting how his arm squeezed around her waist. She rested her hands on his chest, her fingers curling into the soft fabric of his T-shirt. Oh, she could get used to this. Being held by Tate, his arm clamped firmly around her, his fingers perilously close to her backside...

"You dropped your drink," he said.

She couldn't tear her gaze away from his lips. They were full, the lower lip bigger than the top, and she had the sudden urge to touch them.

But she didn't.

"Did I break the glass?" she asked, twisting around to see if she could spot it.

"No. It rolled away. Lost all your champagne though."

"That's…disappointing." She sounded breathless still. Why did he do this to her? Why was he the only one who could do this to her? Every time they were together, electricity seemed to crackle in the air, yet she fought the attraction between them with snarky comments and plenty of eye rolling. She didn't want to feel this way toward Tate. Arrogant fire captains weren't her type. She had a feeling he wouldn't be good for her.

But most of her favorite things weren't good for her. Pizza. Chocolate cake. And any kind of cake, really—she didn't discriminate. Nachos. God, she adored nachos. Oh, and the occasional Frappuccino from Starbucks—those definitely weren't good for her. Booze. Yeah, alcohol wasn't good for her either, yet she'd been chugging champagne like water once that bottle was opened.

Huh. All of the bad things she indulged in were either food or drink, not men. Maybe she was smart, sticking to her no-date-with-Tate policy.

She started to laugh. No date with Tate. That was funny.

"Do you do this on a regular basis?" he asked.

Wren tried her best to contain her laughter, but it was hard. "Do what?"

"Get drunk? I feel like every time I see you lately, you're buzzed."

Well. His words were like a slap of sober reality right to the face. She stepped out of his arms and backed away, needing the distance. "I don't always get drunk."

"Really? Could've fooled me."

He was making her feel like a lush. Like an alcoholic who couldn't control her drinking when she was the furthest thing from that. She drank socially, but that was it.

Except for the time at the bar, when she ran into Tate. Or tonight, when she drowned her pitiful sorrows in champagne. Again, in front of Tate.

She was just having an off week. That was all.

"You seem to catch me at my worst moments," she mumbled, feeling stupid. "I don't normally drink like this."

"I know," he said quietly, his gaze steady and full of understanding. Like he really did know and wanted to be there for her anyway.

His serious expression, how he always seemed to be there for her no matter what, overwhelmed her. She took another backward step, nearly tripping over her dress again, and Tate moved toward her to offer his assistance.

But she held her hands out, stopping him. "I'm fine. Really. I just…I need to get out of here."

Before he could utter a word, she turned.

And ran.

Chapter Seven

"WREN, WAIT!" TATE took off after her, afraid she might do something to hurt herself, like trip over her own feet, or worse, climb into her car and take off.

He didn't like the idea of her doing either of those things, so he chased her down, running around the side of Harper and West's house and pushing through the wooden gate. He jogged across the tiny strip of grass that ran the length of the condos and stopped short when he saw Wren standing on the sidewalk, looking around confusedly before her gaze met his.

"Lost your car?" he asked as he approached her slowly.

She nodded, offering up a little shrug. "I shouldn't drive." Her head dropped, so she was staring at the ground. "There are a lot of things I shouldn't do," she mumbled just loud enough for him to hear.

He stopped beside her, reaching out to slide his fingers along her bare shoulder. She shivered beneath his touch, and for some strangely possessive reason that pleased him. "I'll take you home."

"Do you always rescue damsels in distress?" Wren lifted her head, her smile strained. She looked embarrassed, and he didn't want that. Something was definitely bothering her, but she wasn't comfortable enough with him to open up. And it was clearly something she didn't feel comfortable enough revealing to her closest friends either. He had no idea what was going on inside that head of hers.

And he was sort of desperate to find out.

"The only damsel I want to rescue is you." He meant every word. No other woman interested him. Only Wren. Was it because she didn't like him? That she played so damn hard to get all the time? That she gave him nothing but crap? Though there wasn't any playing when it came to Wren. She didn't like him.

He wanted to change her mind and prove her wrong. He was a good guy when he wanted to be. And she was a challenge, when no other woman had been a challenge for him before…

"So you're my knight in shining armor?"

"If that's what you need me to be."

She contemplated him, tilting her head to the side, her expression unreadable. Her glossy brown hair slid over her bare shoulder and he was tempted to brush it aside. Run his mouth along her skin and taste her with his tongue. But she was buzzed on champagne, and he wasn't going to take advantage of her.

He frowned. Why did this sort of thing always happen between them? Since when did he turn into her rescuer when she was drunk?

"Why are you being so nice to me?" she finally asked. "When I've been nothing but a jerk to you."

"I like feisty women." That was much easier to say than *I like you.*

"When you call me feisty, is that code for bitchy and rude?"

Tate chuckled. "I would never call you bitchy and rude."

"You should. I've been nothing but awful to you since the day we met."

"Why is that anyway? You have something against me or what?" That was the magic question he'd been dying to ask since...the day they met. She'd acted almost hostile toward him that very first time. He'd worn her down a little bit, so at least now when they gave each other shit, some of it was teasing.

But some of it wasn't—at least on her part. He was curious to know what exactly he did to piss her off so thoroughly.

She pressed her lips together, as if she'd already revealed too much. "Where's your car?"

"Over there." He let her subject change slide, figuring she didn't want to talk about it. He was cool with that. After all, she'd be trapped in his car for the next fifteen minutes or so while he drove her home. They could either talk or she could pass out again. Though he wanted her awake tonight. Wanted to see if she was really as drunk as he thought, or maybe she wasn't so buzzed after all.

Why? So you can see if she wants to get busy?

Tate made a face. Even his thoughts sounded stupid.

Without a word, he rested his hand at the small of Wren's back and guided her out into the parking lot toward his car. He'd text West later, letting him know they'd left and apologizing for not saying goodbye.

The night was quiet. He could hear the wind rustle through the trees, the faint roar of traffic down on the main road that circled the lake. The condos were fairly close to Wildwood Lake, though West and Harper's place didn't have that coveted water view.

Wren lifted her face into the breeze as the cool mountain air washed over them, her eyes sliding closed for the briefest moment. "I can smell the pine trees," she murmured, her eyes opening to meet his as they slowed their pace.

"I can barely smell them," he admitted. When he first moved here the smell of all the pines that surrounded the town, the lake, the entire area had almost overwhelmed him. After living in Wildwood for almost a year, he barely noticed them anymore, with the exception of the change of seasons. Those first days of fall, the hushed quiet of winter and the snow that came along with it. The hint of spring and the budding flowers, accompanied by new needles sprouting on the majestic pines.

And those first real warm days of early summer— those were the days most pungent with the familiar piney smell. He imagined the trees braced themselves in preparation for those long hot days, days when there was so much potential for them to be destroyed.

Damn, he was feeling poetic all over a bunch of pine trees. Maybe he was the drunk one.

"You'd think after living here my entire life I wouldn't notice either." Wren shook her head. "But I always can. They're my favorite part of living here. If I moved, where would I find a tree that smells as good as the ones that surround my hometown?"

"If you moved to Oregon or Washington, you could find plenty of pine trees," he pointed out as they drew closer to his car. He pulled the keyless remote out of his front pocket and hit the button to unlock the doors.

"True. I don't think I want to go that far though."

He opened the door for her. "You want to leave Wildwood? Is that what you're telling me?"

She climbed into his car, her gaze meeting his once she was settled in. "I don't know," she admitted. "I've been thinking about it."

Huh. That would change a few things. If she was leaving, then he wouldn't have to worry about her seeking something long term. They could mess around for that brief period of time until she left. No harm, no foul.

He liked the sound of that. A lot.

Slamming the passenger door, he jogged around the front of the car and opened his door, sliding in behind the steering wheel. He started the car, threw it into Reverse, and was about to back out of the spot when Wren reached out and rested her hand on his arm.

Tate met her gaze, taking in her grave expression, how serious her eyes looked. "What's up?"

"I've not told anyone that I want to leave Wildwood. I can barely admit it to myself." She laughed, but it was weak at best. "It's just something I've been thinking about. No firm plans are in place or anything."

He remained quiet, waiting for her to continue. But when she didn't, he said, "Your secret is safe with me."

She squeezed his arm, and he felt that seemingly innocent touch like she'd gripped hold of his cock and stroked him into oblivion. He was hard and aching, just like that.

"Thank you, Tate," she whispered.

"You're welcome, Dove," he whispered back.

Wren didn't even protest the nickname.

THIS TIME, SHE didn't fall asleep in Tate's car. No, she remained wide-eyed and completely awake, which meant she wasn't as drunk as she originally thought. He had an unopened bottle of water sitting in the center console, and she'd drunk half of it in the first five minutes of their drive.

She was trying her best to sober up. For what, she wasn't exactly sure. But anticipation hung in the air between them, like a crackling energy that made her blood hot and her skin tingle. In the hushed confines of his car, it felt as if they were sitting extra close to each other, his thighs spread wide in that way guys sat, his knee reachable. She could reach out and rest her hand on his knee, if she wanted. Slide her hand up the inside of his thigh. Maybe even rub the front of his jeans and see if he had an erection or not...

Her cheeks went hot just thinking about it, and she was glad it was dark. Surely he'd ask her why her face was so red. He'd done that sort of thing before.

"You awake?" he asked.

"Yes. Why do you ask?" God, could he see her blush even in the dark? How embarrassing.

"Last time you were so quiet in my car you were snoring and whispering my name in your sleep," he said.

She went completely still. "I did not."

"You did too. You said my name, and when I asked you who you were dreaming about, you said me." His voice was smug, and she sort of wanted to hit him.

Well, not really. The urge to grab his junk was stronger.

"I have never dreamed about you in my life." Lies.

He chuckled. "It's okay to admit it. I've dreamed about you."

"You have?" She closed her eyes and thunked her head against the back of the seat. Could she sound any squeakier?

"Oh, yeah. Naked, tangled-up-in-each-other-and-the-sheets type dreams." He hit the brakes and came to a stop at an intersection, turning to look at her. His eyes were hooded, and they glittered in the dim light as he watched her, waiting for her reaction. She knew he said that just to shock her, and it worked. The longer he stared at her, the harder she found it to breathe. She saw everything in those pretty green eyes. Heat. Hunger.

All of it aimed directly at her.

"Aren't you afraid I might find that…offensive?" She wrinkled her nose, hoping he'd believe her. He shouldn't.

She didn't think his dreams sounded offensive at all. More like sexy. More like the type of dream she wanted to try to reenact with him, to see if the real thing was just as good.

"Everything I say you usually find offensive. So what's the point in holding back?" He hit the gas, his SUV lurching forward and making her chest jerk against her seat belt. "Do you remember your dream about me?"

"No."

He made a tsking noise. "That's too bad."

She agreed wholeheartedly.

"If you could live anywhere, where would it be?" He asked the question casually but she could tell he was digging for information. She was fine with it too. She'd already confessed her deepest, darkest secret to Tate, and he promised he'd never tell a soul. She believed him. So why not spill everything?

"San Francisco," she answered, nibbling on her lower lip the moment the words slipped out. She'd never admitted that to anyone before. Not her friends, not her family, no one.

"Why San Francisco?"

"It's a beautiful city. When I was a little kid my parents would take us there, and I always dreamed of living there."

"It's expensive."

"I know."

"And crowded."

"I can handle it." Was he arguing with her on purpose?

"I grew up in Berkeley."

She turned in her seat to look at him, shock coursing through her veins. "You did?"

He nodded, never taking his gaze off the road. "My parents both work at the university."

"Shut up. UC Berkeley?" She hadn't said those words in a long time, and they felt foreign, almost like they tripped off her tongue and fell into the atmosphere.

Levi had gone to UC Berkeley. He'd dumped her to have the full college experience, as he'd phrased it to her that night. She'd heard enough rumors to know he'd maxed out the college living too. Joining a frat, partying hard, and nearly flunking out.

"Yeah. I was their biggest disappointment." He shook his head. "Couldn't get in."

"Shut. Up." She started to laugh. "Me either!"

"You wanted to go to Cal?" He sounded shocked.

Should she tell him the real reason she tried to get in there? So she could flaunt herself in front of Levi and remind him of what he'd lost? No, she sounded pitiful even in her own head. "I applied all over California but specifically targeted colleges close to the Bay Area."

"Did you get into any of them?"

"No." This was the painful part. "I got into Fullerton and Fresno State but couldn't get enough scholarship money to pay for it all."

"Not even grant money? Student loans?"

"I was a dependent on my parents' tax returns. They made too much money for me to qualify for much of anything, and they really couldn't afford to pay for my tuition. So I went to the local community college and got

my associate's degree." Lame. It embarrassed her that she didn't graduate college. Harper had. Delilah hadn't, but she owned her own business. Wren may have invested in Delilah's studio, but she wasn't a full partner yet.

She wasn't much of anything yet, and that stung. More than she cared to admit, especially to herself.

"What about you? Were your parents really disappointed you couldn't get in?" she asked when he didn't say anything.

"They knew deep down I didn't want to go. I wasn't cut out for school. Not college at least. I could hold my own and my grades were decent, but I wasn't a brainiac like them. I preferred being outdoors, playing sports, working hard. I hated living in the city. I would've given anything to grow up in a town like this."

How funny. She would've given anything to get out of this town. "Always wanting what you can't have?"

He shot her a glance. "Something like that."

"But you finally got your wish. Now you live here."

"I love it, too. Wildwood is a great town. I love my job. I feel lucky."

"More like hard work got you here, I'm thinking."

"Says the battalion chief's daughter."

Ugh. Her father always had to come back into it. "My father's retired."

"You know what it's like though, living with a firefighter. How they're always gone, especially in the summer."

"Sometimes working, sometimes not," she muttered under her breath. God, she really didn't want to stroll

down memory lane and reminisce about her father's affairs. Didn't Tate know the background story about Wayne Gallagher? Hadn't someone filled him in by now?

She knew this—she didn't want to be the one to have to tell the story.

"What did you say?" he asked.

Wren shook her head. "Nothing important. So why couldn't you get into Berkeley, even with your parents working there?"

"My grades weren't good enough, and my parents said I had to earn it. I didn't, so I signed on as a seasonal fire-fighter the summer after I graduated high school."

"Your parents sound tough," she said.

"They are, but they mean well. I can't even bash them, because I think they're pretty awesome. I'm an only child, so they focused all of their attention on me, hoping I'd turn out just like them, and I so didn't. They're two old hippies who had a child late in life and didn't get what they expected." He laughed.

"I'm guessing they're still pretty proud of you. You're fairly young to already be a captain."

"I became a captain before I was thirty," he said proudly.

"How old are you anyway?" She had no clue.

"Thirty." He chuckled. "How old are you?"

"Twenty-six."

"A younger woman." They drove under a streetlamp just as he grinned at her, and she caught full sight of him and that cute smile. Her heart felt like it flipped over itself. "I happen to like younger women."

She couldn't help the snort that came out. "I'm sure you do." Great. She was so classy.

"Did you just snort at me, Dove?"

"Shut up." She liked how he kept calling her Dove. That was sort of cute. He was being so nice tonight. So…real and open.

"You did snort at me. I like it. Snorting is sexy."

Wren giggled. Actually giggled. She blamed the champagne. "You're full of it."

"Just about anything you do I find sexy. That's no lie."

The seriousness she could hear in his voice caused her laughter to slowly die.

"You're just joking." She paused, and he glanced in her direction, his brows furrowed. "Right?"

He remained quiet as he continued to drive, drawing closer and closer to her place. Damn it, he needed to say something, even if it was *yeah, I'm totally joking*. She wanted to be put out of her misery.

"Holy shit," he breathed, hitting the brakes so hard the car screeched to a stop. "Is that your place?"

She turned in the direction he was staring, her eyes going wide when she saw what he referred to. It was definitely her little cottage.

Fully engulfed in flames.

Chapter Eight

"OH MY GOD!" Wren burst out of the passenger door of Tate's SUV, running toward the small cluster of fire engines that were parked directly in front of her house. Firefighters were everywhere, hoses aimed at the burning building, but even she could tell the damage was total. Flames shot out through the roof and the windows, a column of thick black smoke filling the sky. She stood gaping at the unbelievable spectacle before her when someone grabbed hold of her from behind, clasping her shoulders and giving her a shake before she was whirled around.

"*Wrennie.* Thank God you're all right."

She blinked her baby brother into focus, the stricken look on Holden's face, the worry in his blue eyes. He crushed her into a quick but fierce hug, her face smashed against his chest and the yellow turnout coat he wore before he shoved her away from him.

"Stay back," he warned her with a finger in her face. For once in his life he got to tell her what to do. Any other moment he'd probably relish it too. "We've been trying to call you for the last thirty minutes."

It hit her that she left her phone, her purse, everything back at Harper and West's. "I don't have my phone with me," she admitted, her voice soft, guilt swamping her.

"I was fucking scared you were stuck inside." His expression was grim. He glanced over his shoulder at what was left of her house before he turned back to look at her. "I gotta go. You have someone with you, right?"

"She does." Tate materialized out of nowhere, his big hand resting on her shoulder, his grip firm and reassuring. "I'll take care of her."

Recognition dawned in Holden's eyes and he nodded his greeting to Tate. "Okay, cool. You're in good hands, then," Holden told her before he directed his next words at Tate. "Maybe you could get her out of here? There's no point in Wrennie sticking around tonight." The pointed look he sent Tate said it all.

Her house was a lost cause. Everything inside it, everything she owned, was gone. Up in smoke. Literally.

Her knees wobbled a little bit, and her head spun. "Um…" She tried to speak, but she couldn't get past the lump in her throat. She tried to swallow it down, tried to say something, anything, but nothing came out.

"Dove. You okay?" Tate's voice was close. So close and deep and calm, much like the hand on her shoulder. His fingers squeezed, trying to tell her it was going to be all right with just a touch.

But it wasn't going to be all right. She'd just lost *everything*. The only things she had were what she left the house with this evening.

"No," she croaked out, her voice scratchy, her vision blurring. "I'm not okay."

Tate tugged on her shoulder and she turned to face him. Instead of two eyes he had four, and she blinked hard, trying to bring him into focus. "Wren," he snapped, his voice loud, making her wince. "How many fingers am I holding up?"

She shook her head, but that only made it spin harder. And blinking slowly was no help either. "I don't know. One? Are you flipping me off, Tate?"

That was the last thing she remembered saying.

"Wren. Baby, wake up."

His voice was soft. Full of concern. She smiled, loving that it was directed at her. She turned her head to the side and sighed, her lips curving in the barest smile. The bed she was in was soft and snuggly. The pillow felt like a cloud and the blanket that covered her was warm but not too heavy. She could totally relate to Goldilocks.

Everything was just right.

"Wren. You've been sleeping all night. You need to wake up."

"Don't wanna," she mumbled, turning over on her side so her back was facing whoever was talking.

Whoever? Yeah, right. She knew exactly who was talking. Tate. What was he doing in her dream anyway? And why was he trying to wake her up? It wasn't fair. He got to have dreams where they were tangled up in each other, and she had dreams where he was being a jerk and trying to wake her up. Talk about a party pooper.

"Dove. Someone is here to talk to you. About the fire."

The fire.

Her eyes sprang open, and she stared at the beige wall, frowning at the choice of paint color. It reminded her of a hospital…

She flipped onto her back and sat straight up, pushing her hair away from her face as she glanced around. Relief flooded her when she realized she wasn't at the hospital at all, but a rather empty and very boringly decorated bedroom.

Tate sat in a chair that was pulled up right next to the bed.

"Where am I?" she asked, glancing down, her hair falling in her face. She shoved it back, an irritated noise escaping her as she frowned at what she wore. An over-size white T-shirt with the word *Cal* emblazoned across the chest, written in a blue cursive script. She had no idea where it came from.

"My spare bedroom. You don't remember coming back home with me last night?"

She shook her head but stopped with a wince. Wow, that hurt. Maybe she had more champagne than she remembered. "What time did we come back here?" Not that the time mattered. Lord, did they *do* anything? And she somehow forgot *that*?

Man, she really hoped not.

"We didn't…" Her voice drifted, and she gestured between the two of them, then waved her finger in a circle at the bed.

Tate shook his head. "No. Nothing like that."

"Oh." She felt stupid for even asking. "Okay. Uh, good." Right. If they were going to mess around, she wanted to actually remember it. Too bad they didn't at least kiss. Kissing was good, and she missed it. Missed kissing someone with warm, damp lips and a skilled tongue and wandering hands…

Focus, Wren!

"Do you remember fainting?" When she didn't answer, he pushed for more. "The fire?"

"I remember the fire." Her voice was hollow. Sort of how she felt inside.

Empty.

"You fainted, and I caught you. You were pretty much out of it the entire drive here, and I half walked, half carried you inside." He grabbed hold of her hand and she flinched, shocked at the spark of heat that flamed between them. "You really don't remember?"

She wracked her brain, trying to piece it all together. The fire was burned into her memory—no pun intended—and the fear combined with relief she remembered seeing in her brother's face when he found her. The realization that she'd lost all of her belongings, her house, everything. How overwhelmed she'd felt. How lost.

"Sort of," she finally said, shrugging one shoulder. "Am I wearing your shirt?"

"Well, yeah." When their gazes snagged, he offered her a tiny smile. "I helped you change into it."

Oh, great. That meant he saw her pretty much naked because she wore no bra—she didn't even own a freaking bra now—and the tiny panties she remembered slipping on last night were truly a waste of fabric.

"I saw nothing," he reassured her, like he could read her mind. "I pulled the T-shirt over your head and it fell to about midthigh. Then I just tugged your dress off from beneath the shirt and pushed you into bed."

"Really?" She sounded skeptical, but come on. This was Tate she was talking to. He was always making sexual innuendos at her expense.

"Scout's honor." He crossed his heart with his index finger. "I didn't see a thing."

Any other morning she would've laughed. She would've secretly wished he'd seen *everything*. She might've even whipped his T-shirt off and given him a glimpse of what he missed—if she was feeling particularly brave.

But she was experiencing none of those things now. Not a one of them. Instead, all she could feel was this foreboding sense of despair. Emptiness. She had nothing to her name other than her car, her purse, and her phone.

Tears threatened, and her eyes stung. She closed them tight, not wanting to cry. Willing the tears to go away, she sucked in a shaky breath and told herself to get it together.

Hold it together.

"I know you probably don't want to deal with this right now, but Josh is here. He wants to talk to you," Tate said, his voice gentle. He could probably see that she was on the verge of completely falling apart.

She opened her eyes to find him watching her closely. "Who's Josh?"

"An arson investigator from headquarters. He wants to talk to you about last night. See if you can remember anything."

"I don't know…" Her voice drifted, and she glanced down, realizing that her fingers were still entwined with Tate's. She gave them an experimental squeeze, and he squeezed them back, his touch gentle, his rough fingertips rubbing against hers and making her stomach warm and fizzy.

"It's best if he talks to you now, when your memory is still fresh," Tate said.

Ha. Her memory felt like it was packed full of cotton. White and gauzy and hard to see through. "I'm probably no help. I wasn't there when it started."

"He just wants to ask you a few questions."

Sighing, she lifted her head, her gaze meeting Tate's once more. "You'll go out there with me?"

He nodded.

"I don't have anything to wear." She pressed her lips together. *Don't cry.*

"Slip your dress on under the T-shirt."

"I'll look stupid."

"Josh doesn't care what you look like, Dove. He just wants to talk to you. That's it."

Tate was right. She was being silly. Nodding reluctantly, she let go of Tate's hand and he sprang from the chair as she eased herself off the bed. He brought her dress to her, handing it over. "I'll tell him you'll be out in a sec."

"Okay." She swallowed and made a face. God, her mouth tasted terrible. "Do you have a spare toothbrush maybe?"

"Yeah. Use my bathroom, which is right off my bedroom. Second drawer on the right side I have a pack of extra toothbrushes. Toothpaste is in the top drawer. Take your time." He offered her a gentle smile before he left.

She glanced around the bare room one more time, taking in the tiny white dresser, the spindly chair, the bed that couldn't be bigger than a double. The room was very sparse, the thin white blinds covering the window downright sterile. Clearly the man hadn't bothered to decorate this room. She didn't know if that was a good sign or a bad one.

If it was fully decorated with knickknacks and crap, that meant a woman had done it. Guys don't care about things like that. Not really.

Yeah. She'd take it as a good sign.

Stepping into her dress, she pulled it up until she was fully covered, then decided to yank off the T-shirt and leave it on the bed. Not before she brought it to her nose and gave it a delicate sniff though. It smelled like him, and she breathed in deep, feeling like some sort of creepy stalker with a serious Tate fetish.

Clearly losing all of her earthly possessions in a fire did strange things to a woman.

Wren snuck down the short hall and into Tate's bedroom, closing the door quietly behind her. She glanced around, noticing that this room at least had some character. It reminded her of Tate for some reason, though there weren't a lot of personal belongings in the room that she could see. No photos anywhere of friends or family, though there were plenty of photos featuring familiar landscapes she recognized, of the mountains and lake that she called home.

The photos were fabulous. She wondered who the photographer was.

The bathroom was clean, no signs of womanly products anywhere. She found the packet of toothbrushes—she recognized a Costco special when she saw one—and tore out a pink-handled brush, figuring Tate would never use it anyway. She dug up the toothpaste in the top drawer and brushed her teeth extra hard, feeling the need to brush away all the grime and grit like it was negativity she could banish with a few minutes of scrubbing. A shower would be good, but she'd end up soaking under the hot spray for far too long, and that Josh guy might wonder what was taking so long.

Hopefully she could take a shower after he left.

She chanced a look at her reflection in the mirror and winced. Her hair was a mess, and remnants of mascara were smudged below her eyes. She wet her finger and wiped the leftover makeup away before smoothing down her hair as best as she could.

It would have to do.

Taking a deep breath, she exited Tate's room and ventured out into the living room, where the most intimidating man in full Cal Fire uniform waited for her. He rose from the couch the second he saw her, approaching with his hand stuck out for her to shake.

"Josh Bailey. You must be Wren." His expression was dead serious. "I'm sorry about what happened last night."

They'd encountered each other before, at a barbecue West and Harper hosted a few weeks ago. "Thank you. Nice to meet you. Again." Even in her time of trouble, she was polite. Her mama would be proud.

Oh God, did her parents know what happened? She needed to call them, let them know she was all right. And her friends. Everyone was probably worried sick about her. She needed to reach out to everyone as soon as this interview was over.

She really hoped it wouldn't take too long.

"Sit down." Tate was suddenly there, right beside her, guiding her toward an overstuffed leather chair that faced the couch Josh had just been sitting on. She sat down, looking up at him as he frowned at her. He looked upset. Worried. Was there something more going on that she didn't know? "You want something to drink?"

"Do you have coffee?" She desperately needed the caffeine to bring her back to life. She was still feeling a little groggy.

"Yeah, I can brew you some. Give me a minute." He leaned over her, his hands braced on the armrests and his mouth right at her ear. Completely surrounding her. "You don't mind if I'm in the kitchen? You wanted me to sit with you while Josh asked you questions."

"No, go. It's fine." She offered him a brave smile to prove she was all right with it. And she was.

Sort of.

"I won't be far. Call me if you need me." He lifted away from her and turned to Josh, his voice stern. "She's all yours, but go easy on her. She's had a rough night."

Wren watched Tate go to the kitchen, shocked by his overprotective manner. Who knew he could really be her hero? His gruff hovering was kind of a turn-on.

"I know you're probably still in shock over what happened, so I won't take up too much of your time," Josh said.

She turned her attention to him and smiled. "I'll try my best to answer whatever questions you have."

"Great. I'm going to record this. Hope you don't mind." He hit a button on his phone and spoke into it, noting the date and time and to whom he was speaking. "Can you tell me what time you left your home yesterday, Miss Gallagher?" He recited her address for the record.

"I was gone most of the day and came back around four or four thirty? I took a shower and changed, eventually leaving the house around six. I had a dinner party to go to," she explained.

"Right, at Harper Hill and Weston Gallagher's home." Josh nodded. "Did you see anything or anyone suspicious during the approximately two hours that you were home yesterday afternoon?"

She frowned, trying to recall if she might've seen anything strange, but she knew she hadn't. It had been a normal day. "Not at all. I live on a pretty isolated road with hardly any neighbors. I'd notice if there was something—or someone—unfamiliar lurking about."

"How about when you were getting ready. Did you leave anything on? A curling iron or a straightener? Anything like that?"

"No, not at all. I'm paranoid about leaving that stuff even plugged in." She smiled faintly. "I'm a firefighter's daughter. I just…I'm really cautious. Always."

"Right. Understandable." Josh paused for a moment, angling his head to the left. "So when you arrived at your house last night, Fire Captain Tate Warren was with you, correct?"

"He drove me home, yes."

"And you saw no one else on the road, no other cars passing you by, coming from the direction of your place?"

"No." She shook her head. "The road was quiet. It was late, almost ten. All I remember is seeing the flames shooting up from my house and running toward the fire engines." She breathed deep, trying to call up more. "I ran into my brother Holden. He wanted me to leave though. So did Tate. That's when I think I fainted. After that, I don't remember much." She sent Josh an apologetic look. "I'm sorry."

He smiled, though his gaze remained grim. "Don't apologize. You've given me some good information, now that I know when you arrived home and then left."

Josh rose to his feet and she did the same, surprised that the interview was that short. He shook her hand again. "Thanks for talking to me so soon after the incident. I'll probably need to speak with you again in the next few days."

"That's fine," she said, offering him a faint smile.

Tate came out of the kitchen and escorted Josh to the door, both men talking in low murmurs before she heard the door open and close. Within seconds Tate was in the living room standing in front of her.

"You okay?"

Wren nodded. "It wasn't that bad."

"He knows you didn't see much. They're trying to figure out who's doing this."

"Doing what?"

"Setting all of these fires. I'm thinking it was arson, Wren. Your house was set on fire. On purpose."

Chapter Nine

"THERE'S A LOT you need to take care of," Tate said gently, his gaze fixed on the top of Wren's head, which was bent over the table. She'd been quiet all morning, not that he could blame her. She had to be in a state of shock, considering her house just burned to the ground.

"I know," she mumbled, toying with her silverware. He'd taken her out to breakfast, knowing it wouldn't necessarily cheer her up, but he had to get her out of the house. He wanted to be there for her. Help her out. Dealing with the fire's aftermath was difficult. There was so much to do, so much to prepare.

And it was obvious Wren didn't know where to start.

"You had insurance?" Tate asked her as he stared at his phone. He was in the notes section, making a list of everything Wren needed to do.

"I didn't own the place," she admitted, her voice so soft he almost couldn't hear her. "I rented it."

"But you had renter's insurance." He lifted his gaze to meet hers, but she wouldn't look at him. "Aw, Dove."

She shook her head fast, still refusing to look at him. "I can't talk about it. Not right now. Later, okay?"

Shit. He thought she might be starving, but she only picked at her food. The few locals who were in the place approached their table, checking on Wren, asking if she was all right. She nodded and smiled, acting like everything was going to be okay, but he could tell she was faking it.

She was the furthest thing from okay. Being out in public wasn't helping matters either. He should've picked up something to go or, even better, made her breakfast. But his fridge was pretty much empty, and he was back on shift tomorrow morning, so there hadn't been any reason to stock up.

"I guess I'll have to move in with my parents." Wren pushed her plate away from her, crossing her arms in front of her chest. While she was in the shower, Harper had brought over Wren's purse and phone, along with a change of clothes.

"Do you know where Wren plans on staying?" Harper had asked him when she stopped by.

"Here with me," he'd said firmly, making Harper's eyes go wide with surprise. But she'd never said a word in protest, so he figured she approved.

Not that he cared if he had her approval or not. This was between him and Wren. No one else.

"I want you to stay at my place," he said, holding up a hand when Wren started to protest. She went quiet, and he continued. "I'm going back to work tomorrow, and you'll have the place to yourself. Stay in the spare room, cook in my kitchen, watch TV, whatever you need to do. I don't mind."

She remained quiet, watching him for so long he started to get uncomfortable before she finally said, "Thank you. I appreciate the offer, but I probably…I shouldn't."

"Why not?" He frowned.

"It'll look bad, don't you think?"

"Look bad to who? Everyone else?" He glanced around the restaurant before leaning across the table, his voice lowering. "I don't give a flying fuck what anyone else thinks. You have nowhere to live, Wren. I'm just trying to help a friend out."

"A friend?"

"Isn't that what we are? Friends?"

She shrugged. "I suppose so."

"Right, so who cares what anyone else thinks? You'll stay in my spare bedroom until you get back on your feet." He said it with such finality she smiled and shook her head. "What?"

"You don't really ever back down, do you?"

"Not really," he admitted, sounding almost reluctant. "Not when I know what I'm doing is right."

"So it's right that I should stay with you?" A smile teased the corner of her lush lips, and lust zipped through him. He tamped it down. No way should he think like that, not after what she went through over the last twenty-four hours.

"Where else are you going to go?"

The cute smile disappeared. "Are you doing this because you feel sorry for me? I don't need your pity."

"Dove, you are extremely touchy, and I understand why, trust me. But no, I'm not doing this because I feel sorry for you." He reached across the table and grabbed hold of her hand, intertwining their fingers together. "I want to help you. What happened is the shittiest thing ever. We're going to get whoever did this."

She nodded, removing her hand from his and sinking both of her hands into her lap beneath the table. "I hope you do."

He didn't like how she didn't sound convinced that they could. "Josh and his team are getting closer."

"Not close enough, considering my house just burned down." She bent her head and covered her eyes with her hand, taking a deep breath. "Sorry. I'm just feeling…so many emotions. I can't sort through them all."

Understandable. She'd been through a lot. And now she had nothing, not even renter's insurance. Meaning she lost everything in her house and wasn't going to be compensated for it. Though if she bought anything on a credit card recently she might be able to get some of those items covered…

He'd bring it up to her another time. Definitely not now.

A phone dinged, and Wren reached into her purse, pulling out her cell to read a text. She sent off a quick reply before lifting her gaze to his. "Dee said she found my gym bag at the studio and there were some clothes in it. Including underwear." Her cheeks colored the slightest bit.

"Good. Your friends are going to take you shopping?" he asked.

She nodded and stuffed her phone back in her purse. "Not like I have a lot of time. I need to work to earn money so I can afford all those new clothes and other things, you know?"

Her face crumpled, and he was afraid she'd start crying again. He felt like an asshole every time a tear slid down her cheek because he didn't know what to do or what to say to make it better. Her tears made him feel helpless.

And he hated that.

"You're going to have to take it just one day at a time," Tate said. "Everything that's happened, everything that you need to do, it's overwhelming. Just…take a deep breath and make a list. Figure out what you can handle and what you can't. And don't be afraid to ask for help."

She dropped her hand and nodded, taking another deep breath, this one shakier than the last. "Right. You're right. I know. I have friends. I have family who'll help me. West has already called me twice. Harper too. And Delilah said she's going to bring my bag by your place later. I hope that's okay."

"Of course it's okay." Like she had to ask.

"Okay. Good." She sniffed and grabbed her water glass, taking a long drink. "I can do this. Right?"

"Right."

"My friends will help me. First thing up, I need to find a new place to live." She smiled, though it didn't quite reach her eyes. "That way I'll get out of your hair as soon as possible."

He had no idea how to tell her he didn't mind having her "in his hair"—in his house, in his life. He liked it. Too much.

"No rush," he said easily, leaning back against the booth seat. "Take all the time you need."

Her puzzled expression was cute. Everything she did was cute. He shouldn't think this way, feel this way, but damn it, he *liked* Wren. And his timing with all of these *feelings* was really fucking inconvenient.

"The fire season is almost over," she pointed out.

"So?"

"That means you'll be home more. You won't want me there."

He wanted her there more than he'd ever let her know. Didn't that realization confuse the hell out of him? "It's the end of August."

She nodded. "Right."

"And we're in California. Summer's gonna hang on through September, most likely into October. You know what it's like. You grew up here. Was your dad home much in September?"

"Well. No," she said reluctantly.

"How about October?"

"Sometimes. Sometimes not."

"Exactly. So you hanging out at my place won't be a problem."

"I won't cramp your style?" she asked, making a face.

"Cramp my style?" he repeated. What was she talking about?

"Yeah. With girls or whatever. Women you want to bring home." Her cheeks went bright pink.

Ah. Didn't she get it? Guess not. "Dove. The only woman I want to bring home is sitting across the table from me. And I'm lucky enough that she's going to be actually *living* in my home for the foreseeable future."

"Temporarily," she added, her cheeks even brighter.

"Temporarily," he agreed.

"Okay." She swallowed hard. He caught the delicate movement of her throat, knew he was making her nervous.

Great. They were on equal footing. She made him nervous too.

"But I think you know how I feel about you."

Her gaze met his once more. "How do you feel about me, Tate?"

He shook his head, pushing his empty plate away from him. "I'm not going there. Not right now, after everything you've been through. We can talk about it another time, when you're ready."

"All right," she said, but the disappointment on her face was clear.

And he hated that he was the one who put it there.

THE LAST FEW days had been nothing but a whirlwind of paperwork, interviews, phone calls, and Internet searches. Wren had even managed to put in a few hours at the studio, calculating the month-end expenses and sending out the monthly statements to all the dance families, including the new ones. Delilah had held an open house a few weeks ago to encourage new students to sign up, and Wren had helped her. It had been a great success, and they'd added ten new students to the dance roster.

It may not sound like much, but for their little town? Ten new students were a lot.

But with new students came a new schedule, new shoe orders, new clothes orders—and that all added up to a lot of work. Work she was desperately behind on.

"It's all good," Delilah said as she glanced over the shoe order form. The list for new jazz shoes and ballet slippers was impossibly long. "I'll order the shoes, so take that off your plate."

"Thank you," Wren said, crossing that task off her list.

"So how's it going with…everything after the fire?"

Wren shrugged. She really didn't want to talk about it, but how could she explain that to one of her best friends? She was only asking out of pure concern and love for her. Wren would sound like a snippy bitch if she brushed off Delilah's question. "I went back to the house a few days ago. Holden and my mom took me there."

"Oh." Delilah seemed like she didn't know what to say either. "How was it?"

Fucking awful. That's what Wren really wanted to say. Her every possession was ruined. Thankfully she'd left all her childhood keepsakes and photos at her parents' house. But everything else? It was gone.

Burned to a crisp.

"Everything's gone," she said instead. "It's all been reduced to nothing but ashes and burnt-out hunks of junk. I have nothing."

"You still have your car," Delilah pointed out.

"That's one good thing."

"And you have us." Delilah stood and walked around the desks, kneeling beside Wren so she could wrap her arm around her shoulders. "We'll take care of you."

Wren leaned her head against Delilah's. "I appreciate that. I really do." What would she have done without them? Dee and Harper had already given so much, and she was so thankful for their generosity.

"How is it staying at Tate's place? You two getting along okay?" Delilah asked once she settled back into her desk chair.

"He hasn't been around for us to not get along, so everything's fine." He'd worked pretty much the entire time she'd been there, but he would be home tomorrow.

And she was sort of nervous about it.

"He's such a good guy to step up and help you out like that. I fully planned on having you stay with me, but he insisted," Delilah said.

"Really? He *insisted*?"

"Oh, yeah. Like, he wouldn't even let me talk about it. You were staying with him, end of story."

"Huh." He was rather demanding when it came to watching over her. The feminist within her didn't like it. She could take care of herself, thank you very much. She didn't need a macho man to tell her what to do or where to stay.

But the girly girl buried even deeper *liked* that he wanted to take care of her. Appreciated his insistence that she would stay with him, that he was so incredibly protective. His behavior was so very…archaic yet sexy too. What woman didn't want a man to take care of her sometimes?

Hmm, strong women who believed in themselves and didn't need a man to validate their existence, that's who. Though she liked that he wanted to help her. Protect her. He made her feel safe.

And she really needed that right now.

"Maybe staying with him will bring the two of you closer together." Delilah had the nerve to actually wiggle her eyebrows at her.

Wren shook her head. "It's not like that." But it so was. He said so himself. He was interested in her. The only woman he wanted was living in his house—direct quote. At the time, she'd not given it much thought, her brain too consumed with all the other bullshit she had to deal with.

But late at night, when she was alone in Tate's house, lying in the tiny bed in his guest room, she thought about that moment in the restaurant. The heat she'd seen in his eyes, the deep timbre of his voice when he said he wanted her at his place.

"Whatever you say," Delilah teased, her voice breaking through Wren's Tate-filled thoughts. "But just…be careful."

The teasing tone was gone, replaced by caution. Wren frowned. "What do you mean?"

"It's just… Tate. He's a really nice guy. He's funny, he's hot, and he's easy to talk to. Very charming. I also think he really loves the ladies."

"I'm not stupid, Dee. I know he's a player."

"Yeah well, it's easy to fall under the player's spell if you let yourself. You're going to be spending a lot of time with him," Delilah said. "I don't want you to get hurt by him."

"I won't. Trust me. I know what I'm dealing with."

Wren thought about what she said to Delilah the entire drive back to Tate's place. He practically lived right in town, and she liked being much closer to everything. It used to take her almost twenty minutes to drive home from the studio, but now it took her only five. She could get used to that.

But she didn't love what Delilah had warned her about, or her own reaction. Did she really know what she was dealing with? *Who* she was dealing with?

That would be a no.

The moment she got home, she climbed into the shower in the master bath. Wren knew she should use the other bathroom. It had a perfectly good shower and was directly across the hall from her room, but…

She preferred using Tate's shower. Using Tate's shampoo and soap, imagining him in the shower with her. His bare skin slick with suds and her hands wandering everywhere…

Her imagination was in overdrive, as was her libido. Spending so much time in Tate's home was like playing pretend. The fact that he wasn't around was sort of weird, but it also gave her plenty of time to explore.

Not that she'd invaded his privacy. Oh, no. She wasn't rooting through the stuff in his bedroom or going through personal items. But after spending a few days alone in his house, she got a sense of who he was as a person just by being observant.

First, he was relatively clean. There weren't clothes all over the floor, and his laundry basket wasn't overflowing. There weren't any disgusting smells in the house, which was a total bonus. His bathroom wasn't gross, and he seemed to use his dishwasher on a regular basis. All good signs.

Second, he liked landscape photos. He had quite a few hung on his walls throughout the house, most of them taken locally. She really needed to ask him who the photographer was.

There were also a few personal photos in his living room. One of him standing in the middle of two people she assumed were his parents, another of a group of coworkers in their Cal Fire uniforms, including her brother Holden, and a third of him as a little boy with a dirty face and holding up a fish he must've just caught. He was adorable.

No surprise.

Third, he liked dark colors. The towels in his bathroom were charcoal gray. His comforter was navy blue. The granite countertops in his kitchen were black, though his cabinets were stark white. The walls in his living room were painted a rich, bluish gray and even his couch was dark gray. It all flowed together, simple yet modern, and she appreciated his decorating style.

Though he'd probably get all macho on her and deny he had *any* sort of decorating style.

She liked everything she discovered, especially the photos of him as a little boy and with his parents. It showed he knew where he came from and wasn't embarrassed about it. That he loved his parents and probably thought he was a pretty funny-looking kid.

Could she totally fall for a guy even though he wasn't around? It seemed that way. The more time she spent in his home, the more she liked him. She'd never experienced anything like this before, and she was almost afraid for him to return. How could she go from thinking he was a total player jerk face to a possibly great guy practically overnight? Had she judged him too harshly? Was she making up details about Tate because he'd been gone for a few days, only to have him return and ruin the fantasy?

She was being ridiculous, worrying about what Tate might or might not be. She just needed to let things happen.

Once she climbed out of the shower and dried herself off, she wrapped the thick gray towel around her and went to the counter. She wiped at the fogged-up mirror before she started applying all the usual lotions and creams she needed to function in life. Since Delilah was a Sephora VIB Rouge member, she was able to get all of Wren's favorites shipped to her extra fast, for which she was eternally grateful. Wren braided her hair, slipped on a pair of panties and one of Tate's T-shirts—another one of her secret indulgences when he wasn't around—then went to the kitchen and made herself a grilled cheese sandwich.

Her phone dinged as she sat at the kitchen counter, and she checked her messages, her heart racing when she saw who it was.

Tate.

I'm coming home tomorrow morning.

A smile curled her lips as she reread his message. Maybe if she squinted hard enough it could almost be like they really did live together.

I know. The house is a mess. I'm going to spend all night cleaning it up.

His reply was immediate.

Are you serious???!!!

She laughed and typed.

No, I'm kidding. The place is as immaculate as you left it.

Good. I was afraid I'd have to knock a few points off.

You're using a point system with me?

I use a point system for all the women in my life.

Wren wrinkled her nose. Ew. That was sort of sexist of him.

Okay, fine. That was totally sexist of him.

Even your mom????

Gross, never my mom.

She laughed and shook her head, getting ready to answer him when another text appeared.

Right now you top the list.

What list?

My points list. You're at 100/100.

Her heart flipped over itself. So stupid. He just admitted to using a points system and rating women, and she was happy because she had a perfect score? What the hell was wrong with her?

I'm honored.

You should be. No other woman has scored that high.

Wren nibbled on her lower lip. They were totally flirting. Not sexting, but this was some major flirtation going on.

How do I rate so special?

You're just…

She frowned, watching the gray conversation bubble appear, the little dots showing that he was texting. Then they stopped. Started up again. But still no reply.

She was just…what?

"Ugh." She set the phone down and dumped her paper plate in the trash, refilled her water bottle, and went back to her phone to see if he'd responded yet.

He had—with one simple word.

You.

Oh. *Wow.* That was the simplest yet sweetest thing a guy had ever said to her. Or maybe she was making more out of this than she should. This wasn't a big deal, right? Was she making it more of a big deal?

Her phone dinged again.

What are you doing?

I just ate dinner.

Me too.

A pause. Another text.

What are you wearing right now?

Wren glanced around like someone could see her. She was being ridiculous.

Um, I don't know if I should tell you.

If you're naked, just break it to me gently. I'm in a roomful of people right now.

She laughed again and shook her head.

I'm not naked. I just…might've taken something that doesn't belong to me.

Isn't that pretty much everything you're wearing and using right now?

Jerk. Though he was right, so she couldn't be mad at him.

What if it's something that belongs to YOU? Would you be mad?

You're wearing something of mine?

She was embarrassed to admit it. Felt like she was opening herself up to him when she should probably hold back.

Maybe.

His response was immediate.

Tell me.

Instead of telling him, she thought she'd show him. She opened up her camera, hit the icon that flipped it into selfie mode, and snapped a photo of her with no makeup, her hair in a wet braid, and wearing Tate's shirt. She hit Send before she could second-guess herself, then immediately second-guessed herself.

You're wearing my shirt. Tell me you're naked underneath it.

Wren pressed her thighs together. She was definitely getting worked up over his flirtatious texts.

I'm wearing panties. No bra.

Her phone rang, startling her, and she answered it. "Hello?"

"You're fucking killing me."

She pressed her lips together to try to contain the smile that wanted to burst free, but it was no use.

"And right now I know you're laughing or smiling or whatever it is that evil, teasing women do when they purposely set out to drive men crazy," he continued, sounding completely put out.

"I am not."

"You so are." His voice lowered. "You look cute in my shirt."

"I've worn one of your shirts before."

"Because I put it on you. This time you *chose* to wear that shirt. You went into my closet, pulled it off the hanger, and slipped it on." He hesitated. "What were you doing in my closet anyway?"

"Looking for a shirt to wear. I wasn't snooping." She chewed on her thumbnail nervously, hating how defensive she just sounded. "I like your T-shirts. They're really soft," she admitted.

"As soft as your skin?" His low, deep voice made heat unfurl in her belly.

"Tate…" She squirmed, wondering what they were doing, why they were saying these things. Was it safer since they weren't actually in the same room together? Or was he doing this to distract her?

If that was the case, then it was working.

"I have a question." She hesitated, then decided to go with it. "The photos hanging on your wall."

"The landscapes?"

"Yeah. They're beautiful. Who took them?"

"I did."

Wren was surprised. And impressed. "Really?"

"You sound shocked."

"I sort of am." Her voice softened. "They're beautiful."

"Thanks. I used to think I wanted to be a photographer, but now it's just a hobby."

"Well, you're very good."

His voice deepened. "I'm good at lots of things."

A laugh escaped her. "Did you just turn this conversation dirty?"

"Me? Never. So tell me. What are you doing tomorrow?"

"Um…working?"

"Can you take some time off?"

"I make my own schedule, so sure."

"We should spend the day together. You deserve to forget your troubles and have some fun."

She wanted to take him up on his offer, but was it a mistake? Maybe she shouldn't be off messing around and wasting the day away with Tate. There was so much for her to do still. Like look for a place to live. Find more work. Buy more stuff.

"I'd like that," she said. "I do need a break."

"Good. Then I'll see you tomorrow morning." She was about to end the call when she heard him say, "Hey, Dove."

"Yes?"

"Sweet dreams."

Chapter Ten

TATE UNLOCKED AND pushed open the front door, closing it behind him quietly. It was still early, barely past seven in the morning, and he hadn't been so thankful to come home to his own bed in a long time.

Just before midnight his engine had gone out on a medical aid call. It was a multiple car accident on the highway, with the southbound vehicle drifting over the double yellow line and crashing into a car headed north. It had been a nasty wreck; the driver of one car was in critical condition and had to be airlifted to the hospital.

They'd worked through the night and had finally made it back to the station around four. Meaning he got maybe two, two and a half hours before he was relieved from his duties early, and he drove straight home.

He couldn't wait to drive his ass straight into bed.

The guest room door was closed and he figured Wren was still sleeping. He crept into his room and went straight to the bathroom, shutting the door before he turned on the shower. Stripping off his clothes, he got under the hot spray and let it pour over him, washing away the dirt and grime and reminding him that he was so damn tired.

His shower was quick, and he dried off, striding out into his room to grab a pair of boxer briefs to slip on before he climbed into bed.

He stopped short at the sight before him.

A Wren-shaped lump lying in the center of his bed.

Her hand was tucked beneath her cheek, her lips slightly parted and eyes closed, fast asleep. She looked... beautiful.

And he was naked.

Shit.

He went to his dresser and slowly pulled open the top drawer, grabbing a pair of black underwear and glancing over his shoulder. Thank Christ she was still fast asleep. What would she do if she discovered he was standing next to the bed with his dick flapping in the breeze? Be happy about it? Or freak the hell out?

Well, *she* was the one sleeping in his bed like some sort of fairy-tale princess. Or maybe he was thinking of Goldilocks. The girl who ate all the porridge and slept in all the beds until finding the one that was just right.

Why did he have the feeling that Wren could be just right...for him?

Pulling his underwear on, he went back into the bathroom and brushed his teeth, ran his fingers through his wet hair, and contemplated spraying on some cologne.

That would be too obvious. He really just wanted to collapse into bed and fall asleep.

But how could he with Wren in it? Not like he could just snuggle up to her…

Could he?

Nah.

Maybe. She was in *his* bed.

He shut off the bathroom lights and went back into his bedroom, staring at his bed. Wren had rolled over onto her back, her dark hair spread out all over his pillow, the sheets pulled low so he could see she was still wearing his T-shirt. She lay right in the middle of the mattress like some sort of bed hog, and he decided, *fuck it.* He was too tired to think straight, and no way was he taking that crappy guest bed or the couch.

Nope, he was going to sleep in his own damn bed. Catch a few z's for a couple of hours and hopefully feel good as new. Then he planned on taking Wren out and having fun. No thinking about fires or replacing things or trying to find a new place to live. Wren needed a day to get her mind off her troubles. And he was the one who was going to give it to her.

Tate carefully pulled the comforter and sheet back and slipped beneath them, the mattress creaking and dipping under his weight. She stirred at the sound, rolling over so her back faced him and offering him more space. He pulled the blankets over him and lay on his right side, his fingers itching to run through her hair. Test to see if it was as silky as it looked.

So he gave in to his urges and touched her hair. Combed his fingers through it, discovering that yes, it was definitely as silky as it looked, maybe even more so. She made a low murmuring sound and thrust her butt out so it brushed against his front, and he was instantly hard.

Gritting his teeth, he disentangled his fingers from her hair and told himself to get a fucking grip.

His hand snuck out to touch her on her lower back, slipping his fingers beneath the hem of his shirt until he touched bare, warm skin. Closing his eyes, he kept his hand there, smoothing it along her back until his fingers curved over her hip. He scooted closer, pulling her in, until they were snug against each other like two puzzle pieces clicking into place.

She felt good like this. She was warm and soft and smelled so damn good, he leaned in and sniffed her hair, brushing it aside so he could breathe in the scent at her nape. His cock twitched, but he didn't want that. Not yet. He was content to just hold her for now…

Within minutes of sliding into bed he felt Wren stiffen up, and he knew she was awake. He'd just about drifted off to sleep too when her every muscle seemed to freeze. Hell, he wondered if she was even breathing.

"It's okay," he murmured into her hair. It tickled his nose, and he tried to nudge the wild strands out of his face. "Go back to sleep."

"Um…Tate?"

"Yeah, Dove?" He was done running through the various bird names, but Dove stuck. The nickname fit her.

Doves were gentle birds. They were pretty and made soft, cooing sounds. He liked them.

Much like the woman in his bed.

"What are you doing?"

"I should be the one asking you that, right? You're in *my* bed."

"Oh. Right." She sounded almost disappointed.

"Go to sleep," he commanded again, slipping his arm around her so his hand rested just beneath her breasts. He hauled her in even closer, her knees bending to accommodate his, and he closed his eyes.

Though he was afraid he wouldn't get any sleep with her delectable body snuggled so close.

"Are you mad?" she asked after a few quiet minutes.

He sighed, pretending she was putting him out. "Why would I be mad? There's a sexy, warm woman sleeping in my bed. I can't complain."

"An uninvited woman."

"I'd let you in my bed anytime, you know this." He kissed the back of her head, wishing he were kissing her somewhere else. Hell, they hadn't ever really kissed, and he was dying to know the taste of her lips.

"So you're not angry with me?"

"No. I don't mind you rifling through my closet, and I definitely don't mind finding you in my bed. Next time, though, make sure you're naked. That would be a lot more exciting."

She tried to jab him in the ribs with her elbow, but he dodged her just in time. "Rude."

"Ow." He chuckled, enjoying their easy conversation. He felt totally comfortable with her. He liked that they could just talk and there were no expectations. Though if he had expectations, he figured she could deliver on those too, as could he. She wanted him.

He wanted her.

So that made what was brewing between them fairly simple.

"What's on the agenda today?" she asked.

"That's a surprise." He had no idea what was on the agenda. He fully planned on making it up as they went along.

"I like surprises."

"Good, because with me, you're going to get them all the time." An ex from long, long ago had accused him of being too spontaneous. Being thoughtless. Behaving recklessly with her heart.

She was the last of what he called his steady girl-friends. And that had been ages ago. He hadn't had a real girlfriend in years. He was too damn busy to commit. Work came first. He figured he'd have time for a relationship later.

But later was starting to creep up on him. His friends were all pairing off, and they seemed happy. He was tempted to experience some of that happiness too.

With Wren.

"That sounds fun," she said softly, her fingers drifting across his forearm and nearly making his eyes cross. Her simple touch felt so good.

"I'm a barrelful of fun." He sounded like an idiot, but he was too tired to care. "Now please. Close your eyes and go back to sleep."

"Really? That's all you're going to say after you find me in your bed?" She sounded incredulous.

"What do you want me to do? Kick you out? Rip your clothes off? No way am I damaging one of my perfectly soft T-shirts."

She laughed and shook her head, her hair brushing across his face. "You're crazy."

"So are you. Now go to sleep, okay?" He reached up and cupped one of her breasts, making her gasp. "Or should we just forget sleep, and I'll rip the T-shirt off after all?"

Wren was contemplating his suggestion. He could practically feel the cogs turning in her brain. He would've been up for it too. Whatever she wanted, he'd give her. As best as he could, considering how exhausted he was.

"Did you go on a call before you were let off?" she asked.

How did she know? "Yeah."

"You seem tired."

"I am."

"Maybe we should just cuddle then," she suggested.

"I like cuddling." He hadn't done it in forever. She felt good in his arms.

Too good.

"So do I."

"I also like making out."

He could hear the smile in her voice. "Me too."

"We'll have to do that tomorrow though. I'm too tired to kiss you, which is bad. Meaning I won't be giving you my best performance, and that's the least you deserve. So you'll just have to wait." His words became slower, and his head felt heavy.

"I can wait. Anticipation is a lovely thing." Her voice was fading. She sounded so far away.

Tate couldn't bother answering her. He fell asleep to her whispering his name.

WREN BLINKED HER eyes open to find the room flooded with bright sunlight. And a very warm, very…um, *hard* man snuggled up behind her. Tate's hand had somehow snuck beneath her shirt and was cupping her bare breast, her nipple trapped between his fingers. His other hand rested on her hip, fingers curled into the fabric of her panties…

She wiggled her butt against him, secretly hoping that would wake him. Never in her life had she slept so close to a man before. She enjoyed cuddling, but after a few minutes she would push the guy off and that would be that.

With Tate, she was fairly certain they slept exactly like this for the last few hours. And she didn't want him to let her go.

Well, okay, maybe she wanted him to let her go because she had to pee, but that was so completely unromantic and right now should be all about sweet, romantic thoughts.

Or hot and sweaty, sexy thoughts. That had loads of potential…

"I can literally hear you think," Tate murmured against her neck.

Just before he kissed it.

She shivered from the touch of his warm lips on her skin. "What do you mean?"

"You're trying to figure out a way to slip out of bed without waking me."

Unbelievable. "It's really scary how deeply embedded you are in my brain."

He chuckled, his breath tickling her and making her duck away from him. "I've got you figured out. Somewhat."

"You do realize you're touching me in an…inappropriate place." He brushed his fingers against her nipple when he removed his hand from her breast, and she barely repressed the shudder that took over her. "Can I ask you a question, Tate?"

"Whatever you want to know. I'm an open book."

She was so incredibly glad they weren't facing each other. She wouldn't want him to see her face, to look into her eyes. Though with their bodies pressed together so intimately, it was already fairly awkward. She was pretty certain that was his rather aggressive erection nudging against her lower back.

"Are we really going to do this?" She spoke in a whisper, her eyes falling shut when he drifted his fingers along the column of her neck before he pushed her hair away.

"I think we are." He kissed her nape again, his mouth lingering. "But just know that I'm willing. Whatever you want, I'm yours."

Temporarily, she almost added but didn't. She needed to live in the here and now, not worry about the past or freak out over the future. There was plenty to freak out over. Adding worry over Tate and whatever they were doing to the mix wouldn't be smart.

But she was attracted to him. Yes, fine, she wanted him badly. It didn't help that he was wrapped all around her and his mouth was on her neck, her weak spot. Oh, he just nibbled on her skin, and wow, that felt so good…

"Turn around," he demanded, his voice soft.

Reality intruded, and she shifted out of his arms, trying to get away from him. "No way. I have serious morning breath."

"Come on. It can't be that bad."

"It's worse." She slipped out of bed and stood, turning to study the man whom she'd just spent the night with, yet they didn't do anything. Oh, he was so gorgeous it almost hurt to look at him. His dark hair was a disheveled mess and sticking up everywhere. His eyes were heavy lidded and sleepy looking. There was scruff on his cheeks and jaw, and he wasn't wearing a shirt, so all she could see was acres of smooth, male skin stretched over muscle. "I should brush my teeth."

He patted the spot she just vacated, his smile inviting. "You should come back to bed."

"No." Wren shook her head and walked backward, glancing over her shoulder to make sure she didn't trip over anything. "I need to brush my teeth and start some coffee. You should get up and brush your teeth too."

Hopping out of bed had nothing to do with her teeth or getting coffee. It just felt like everything was happening so fast. She needed to put the brakes on it. Get some distance. Gain some brain cells back before she did something really crazy. Like strip naked and jump him.

"You're no fun." He pouted, which was adorable. And she never thought a man who pouted, even in jest, was adorable. But somehow, Tate pulled it off.

"I'm lots of fun. If you're lucky, I'll show you exactly how much fun I am." God, she hoped she could live up to her own personal hype.

"I'll take you up on that." He grinned and climbed out of bed, allowing her a good look at him in his boxer briefs and nothing else. They left little to the imagination, and yep, he had a semiserious case of morning wood happening. "Quit gawking, and go brush your teeth," he teased.

She scurried out of his bedroom before she could say or do something stupid.

Like tackle him to the ground.

Chapter Eleven

THEY STARTED OUT the afternoon running a few mundane errands—she needed to go to the post office to temporarily forward her personal mail to the dance studio, and Tate wanted to stop by the hardware store for a few things. They joked around and he helped take her mind off the disaster that had become her life. He was sweet and kind, and she wondered at first if he had an ulterior motive until she finally realized he was just…

Being himself.

It was dangerous, hanging out with Tate, running errands like they were a real couple and living a life— together. They so weren't. Yes, they were attracted to each other and might end up messing around with each other, but come on. They hadn't even kissed yet. What was he waiting for?

What are you waiting for?

"Where are we going next?" she asked after they got back into his SUV.

He flashed a secretive smile in her direction before returning his attention to the road. "The lake."

She gaped at him. "The lake? Why?"

"First, it's hot as hell today, and I wanted to cool off. Second, you need to do something fun to take your mind off the shit you went through lately. And third, I want to see you in a bikini." His grin was wicked when he said that last bit.

"But I don't have a bikini," she said, her head spinning. He wanted to see her in a bikini? Of course he did. He'd had his hands all over her this morning before, like an idiot, she'd leapt out of his bed and ran away like a chicken. Something would've happened. Something momentous that she'd been too scared to face.

But Tate acted like it never occurred. He'd been easygoing the entire day, never bringing up their extremely close and potentially awkward moment in bed earlier.

Now she sort of wanted to talk about it. Or explore it further.

Okay, fine, she totally wanted to explore it further.

"I have one for you."

She stared at him. "You have a bikini for me?"

He nodded.

"Where'd you get it?"

"I bought it." He shrugged, sending her another quick look. "When you were at the post office? I went to that little clothing store next door."

Items Out Receipt

BPL- East Boston Branch Library
Wednesday, March 08, 2017 4:18:37 PM

Title: No witness but the moon
Material: Book
Due: 3/29/2017

Title: Torch
Material: Paperback Book
Due: 3/29/2017

Title: Everybody's guide to small claims c
ourt
Material: Paperback Book
Due: 3/30/2017

Oh. God. She shopped there often. Did he know her size? What if it didn't fit? What if it exposed too much skin? What if—

"Stop worrying. You're going to look great, and you'll have fun. I promise. We'll hang out at the beach and swim for a little while, and then we'll go grab lunch," he said, his words shutting off her overactive brain.

Well, not quite. She still couldn't stop wondering why he would've bought her a bikini. Or how she might look in it. Or that she'd feel exposed in front of him, and she didn't want to do that. He made her feel exposed enough when she was fully clothed.

In all honesty, he made her feel lots of things she didn't understand, and that left her confused. Always with a look or a joke or a smile, he seemed so at ease around her. So nice. And she'd been nothing but awful, like some sort of weird defense mechanism to push him away.

Instead here they were. Together. Not *together* together, but still. She was staying at his house. He bought her a bikini. He'd wrapped himself around her in his bed while she slept there wearing only his T-shirt.

Everything had just turned…frighteningly weird between them. In a good way.

In a very, very good, very, very confusing way.

She didn't want to like him. She didn't. So…why did she? Because she was in a vulnerable place and he was being so kind?

Her mouth curved into a frown, and she averted her head, staring out the window and watching the world pass by. She hoped he didn't pity her. That he was being so nice only because she had nowhere else to go, which wasn't necessarily true. She had plenty of friends who'd take her in. She could go back and live with her parents.

Her frown deepened. No. Not her parents. That would be the worst.

He pulled into the lake's day-use parking lot a few minutes later, handing over a shopping bag that didn't have much in it after he shut off the engine. She took it with a hasty thank-you and ran to the bathroom to change in one of the shower stalls. Pulling the bikini out of the bag, she admired the pretty, brightly colored floral pattern and was grateful it wasn't made out of string.

Once she got the swimsuit on—oh my God, was she thankful she shaved and recently had a wax—she glanced in the mirror and realized it fit her perfectly. And that Tate had included a cute black cover-up dress she could toss on over the bikini.

He thought of everything.

She exited the bathroom to find Tate waiting for her outside, sunglasses covering his eyes, wearing a pair of tropical print board shorts and nothing else, a bag at his feet stuffed with a couple of beach towels. She tried her best not to stare at his chest, but…

She stared at his chest. Gaped at him, really.

Grinning, he grabbed the bag's handles and slung it over his shoulder. "Ready?"

"Yeah." She snapped her lips shut to keep from drooling. "Thank you for the bikini. And the cover-up. What do I owe you?"

He shook his head and started walking to the lake. She fell into step beside him. "You don't owe me anything. It's a gift."

"But you've already done so much," she started to protest but he shut her up with a look.

Oh, and with the way he grabbed her hand and interlaced their fingers together. "Stop. Just take it graciously, and say, *Thank you, Tate.*"

"Thank you, Tate," Wren said, her voice soft, her fingers tingling from his touch.

She could get used to this sort of treatment.

And that was a scary thought.

TATE TRIED NOT to stare. Really, he did. He was doing his best to be a proper gentleman and be respectful, but damn, it proved hard when Wren tugged the cover-up off over her head and exposed her glorious body. He'd checked her out before, of course.

But this time it was just the two of them alone at the lake, Wren wearing a bikini he bought for her and looking hot as fuck.

He scrubbed a hand over his face. Kept it over his mouth for a few seconds so he wouldn't say something stupid, like, *Fuck me standing, you're gorgeous.* Or, *Hey let's forget all this foreplay bullshit and go back to my place.* Worse, he was tempted to say something desperate and lame, like, *Can I just touch you? Please?*

Yeah. None of that would go over real well. Not with Wren. He felt cautious around her. Like with every progressive step they made, they ended up taking a few steps back. All because he said or did something stupid.

"You coming in?" she called from over her shoulder.

Tate glanced up to watch her head toward the water, her hips swaying gently, her perfect ass barely covered by the bikini bottom. He tore his gaze from her ass because staring at it too long could cause problems. Like, a-tent-in-the-front-of-his-board-shorts problems.

Jesus. He really needed to get a grip.

He followed after her without a word, the cool water splashing around his legs not doing much to cool his heated libido. She'd already dived smoothly into the water, submersing herself completely before popping back up less than a minute later. She smoothed her hair away from her face, water droplets clinging to her eyelashes as she blinked at him, a little smile curving her lips. "This was a good idea."

"I'm glad you approve," he said before he dunked under the water. She said something else, but he couldn't make it out, her words muffled by the water. He stayed under for a while, opening his eyes to see her legs churning, the bright red nail polish on her toes. He noticed everything about her, every little detail, and it was starting to make him realize something.

He had a...thing for her. A thing that wasn't going away anytime soon. And he wanted to know if she could possibly have a thing for him too. Could she? Could she let down her walls and let him in? Not fight him every step of the way? Most of the time he didn't even know what they were arguing about. He was over it.

But he definitely wasn't over Wren.

"Are you part merman or what?" she asked when his head emerged from the water. She scowled at him, like she was pissed, and his defenses automatically went up.

Damn it, he didn't want to spend today like this.

"Why do you say that?" he asked as he slowly swam closer to her. He didn't want to startle her, but he was this close to hauling her into his arms and shutting her up. Kissing sounded like a lot more fun than arguing.

"You were underwater for so long. I, um, got worried." She shrugged one bare shoulder, the water slipping over her skin, and he discovered it was possible to be jealous of water.

Unbelievable.

"You worried about me, Dove?" He treaded water right in front of her, wishing they weren't so deep. He'd rather be standing when he kissed her, but he could make do if needed. "I'm touched."

"You should be. The last thing I need is you drowning on my watch." A smile teased the corners of her perfect lips, and relief hit him hard and swift, nearly taking his breath.

Good. She wasn't mad. She wasn't going to put up a fight. This was going to be a good afternoon. A progressive afternoon. That's what he wanted. What she needed.

"On your watch, huh?" He raised a brow, reaching out and streaking his fingers across her shoulder. She jumped a little, moving away from him, but he just followed. "Aren't I supposed to be the one taking care of you?"

"I can take care of myself."

"I know you can, but right now, you're on my watch." He grinned when she frowned. "Come on, Wren. Throw me a bone here. I'm the big bad firefighter who's come to your rescue. Let me live my fantasy, if just for a little bit."

She laughed, the joyous sound ringing through the air. The lake wasn't too busy. It was a weekday, and not many people came to this beach since it was mostly frequented by the Wildwood locals. They were pretty much alone, with the occasional boat or Jet Skier passing by.

"You have a hero complex?" she teased.

He scoffed. "Of course I do. Why do you think I work this job?"

Her laughter grew. "I figured you tried to drive women crazy in your uniform."

"Do I drive you crazy when I wear my uniform?"

The laughter died. Her expression grew serious. "You drive me crazy when you wear just the board shorts."

His mouth went dry.

"Or when you sneak into your bed and I'm already in it."

His entire body went stiff.

She shook her head, the movement making the water ripple around her. "I should've never admitted that."

"I'm fucking thrilled you just admitted that." He moved toward her, stealth-like and smooth in the water, until he was directly in front of her. He stretched his legs downward, testing where the bottom might be, and was relieved when he actually touched the slightly slimy ground. "I thought I only drove you crazy when I opened my mouth."

A surprised burst of laughter shot from her lips. "You always have your mouth open."

"I know." He smiled. "I could never figure out what I did wrong."

"Did it matter to you that much?"

"It mattered, Dove. You mattered. Your opinion of me."

She looked adorably confused. "Why?"

"Because I like you. And I think you like me too." He reached for her. Slipped his arms around her waist and tugged her in. She didn't fight, didn't protest, just went willingly, her hands automatically going to his chest, her fingers sliding across his skin and sending a scattering of hot sparks through his blood.

"I don't really like you," she said, the words feeling like an automatic response.

"I don't believe you." He slipped his fingers beneath her chin and tilted her face up. "Be truthful with me."

She blinked up at him, little droplets of water clinging to her cheeks, and he wiped them away, his thumb lingering on her soft, soft skin. "I don't know what's happening," she whispered.

"Me either."

"You scare me."

His thumb went still. "In a bad way?"

"No." She shook her head. "In a confused, sexually frustrated way."

It was his turn to laugh. "I think that's a good thing."

"You do?" Her brows scrunched, and he traced the curve of her cheek, the point of her chin.

Tate nodded. "The best possible thing," he murmured just before he leaned in and kissed her. The softest, gentlest kiss. Nothing too pushy, though he wanted to push. He wanted to plunder and taste and conquer and bite and lick.

Instead he pulled away, his smile growing at the dazed look on her pretty damp face. "You want to race?" he asked.

He'd confused her now. "What?"

"Let's race to the floating dock and back." He nodded toward said floating dock, which all the teenagers crowded onto during the weekends. "Loser buys the winner dinner."

She sent him a shrewd look, one full of mysterious, unsaid things. "You're challenging me to a race?"

He nodded.

"The girl who grew up with three of the most competitive brothers in all of Wildwood."

Uh-oh. "Yeah," he said, the uncertainty in his voice distinct.

She grinned. Out and out grinned and thrust her fist into the air. "I've got this. On three?"

"Sure thing," he said and, with a deep breath, started to count.

Wren was gone by the time three slipped past his lips. And she never looked back either. He launched after her, swimming as fast as he could, but he could never catch up to her.

He sincerely hoped that wouldn't be a regular thing.

Chapter Twelve

"ARE YOU HUNGRY?"

Tate's deep voice penetrated her thoughts, and she glanced up, flashing him a small smile. "Starved."

They were back in his SUV after spending a few hours at the lake. Swimming. Lounging on the beach stretched out on the giant towels. Sending secret smiles at each other before they launched into some ridiculous conversation about life or politics or whether Harper and West should elope or not. Always in the back of her mind was that kiss. That one simple yet staggering kiss had seared her from the inside out.

Oh, and left her wanting more, though he hadn't delivered. Damn him.

"Let's go to the BFD for a burger." He sent her a look. "If you're okay with that."

Her smile was smug, considering she won the first swimming race. And the second. The man was a good swimmer, but she was better, after being trained by her brothers her entire life.

"I'm fine with that. You're paying after all." He shook his head and muttered something under his breath, which only made her laugh. And he smiled too, though it was more of a smirk. A cute smirk. He was a little sunburned, his cheeks and nose red, his hair a mess and sticking up everywhere, and wow, she never thought she'd seen him look better.

She sat up straighter when she realized she was staring, but he didn't notice. He was too busy concentrating on driving, which was a good thing. A very good thing. If she'd been driving she probably would've wrecked the car, and the reason would've been so incredibly lame.

Oh, sorry, Lane—because it would definitely be her brother who came upon the accident scene first—*I was too entranced with Tate's male beauty, and I crashed the car.*

Yeah. Lame. So lame.

"I had no idea you were such a good swimmer," Tate said, his gaze still fixed on the road.

"There are lots of things you don't know about me." She sounded flirtatious. The entire afternoon had felt like foreplay. Fun, yummy, sort of sexual but sort of not sexual foreplay. What would happen when they returned to his place? She already felt like she was lit from within. One look from Tate and he sent her into a slow burn. If he touched her again—or even better, kissed her again—she'd probably combust.

"True," he said, his voice low and rumbly. It sent her nerve endings into a quiver. "Though I'd like to find all of those things out."

If she could get away with fanning herself, she would. But she restrained her hands beneath her legs and pretended what he just said hadn't set her on fire.

Lord help her, she was in deep, deep trouble.

They pulled into the BFD parking lot and nerves flapped in her stomach like giant bats. She might run into Harper while they were there, but she could handle it. Right? Harper would most likely make suggestive comments and pull her aside to gush that they made a cute couple, but Wren would just blow her off. Or at least, she should blow her off.

Because whatever they were doing was temporary. He'd helped her forget about the fire and what she lost, but it all came roaring back in this very moment. Heck, she was half-inclined to pack up what little she owned in the world and move somewhere else just because she could. She had no obligations, nothing tying her down besides her various accounting jobs. But she would give enough notice so everyone had time to replace her. Some of the work she could do from anywhere, meaning she wouldn't have to quit at all. She could just…

Be somewhere else.

"Finally." He shifted the car into Park and cut the engine, turning to smile at her. He reached over, touching her cheek, his fingers drifting across her skin, and she pressed her lips together to prevent him from seeing them tremble. "I've had a good time with you today."

His touch rendered her speechless. All she could do was nod.

"Hope to have a good time with you tonight too." His eyes grew dark, and her mouth grew dry.

Temporary. No matter how much fun they were having and how much she was growing to like him—*really* like him—she needed to remind herself of that.

Frequently.

THE MOMENT THEY walked into the restaurant, Wren knew something was up. She could feel it in the air. A sort of electricity that crackled and hummed, though she couldn't place it. Harper's eyes went wide when she caught sight of them, and she rushed over, a fake smile plastered on her face as she steered them toward the doors that led outside to the patio.

"I don't want to eat outside," Wren protested with a shake of her head.

"It's such a nice evening though." The pleading look Harper sent her couldn't be mistaken.

"It's still over one hundred degrees outside," Tate pointed out gently, tipping his head toward the many empty tables in the diner. "We'd rather sit in here. Right, Wren?"

"Definitely," Wren said, surprised that he actually called her by her name. Though he had been all afternoon, throwing in the occasional Dove to balance it out. She didn't mind anymore. Not really.

"I'm going to use the restroom," Tate said to Wren, offering her a gentle smile that she felt all the way down to her toes. "I'll be right back."

The moment he walked away, Harper turned toward Wren, her expression serious, her voice hushed. "You need to get out of here."

"Wait. What?" What was Harper's problem? "Are you refusing to serve us? What the hell, Harp?"

Harper grabbed hold of Wren's arm and pulled her closer to the front of the restaurant where no one else was around. "Someone's here, and I don't want you to see them."

"See who?" Curiosity made her try to look around Harper to see whom she could be talking about.

"Stop looking around! God, you're so obvious." Harper blew out a frustrated breath. "Fine, it's Levi."

Wren went completely still. "Levi? My Levi?" She hadn't referred to him like that in forever. She hadn't thought of him as hers in years. Yet here she was, first mention of him and falling back into old habits. He'd been her Levi once upon a time.

Until he wasn't.

"Yes. He came in a few minutes ago with his parents." Harper sent her a pointed look. "I'm sure you don't want to run into him while you're with Tate."

"I don't mind." The thought actually filled her with excitement. She could show Levi she'd moved on, right? Tate was gorgeous. Even Levi would have to acknowledge that. To look like she was involved with Tate would put on quite the I'm-so-over-you show for Levi. He'd get the message loud and clear.

And she *was* over Levi. She had been for years. Yes, he'd broken her heart in high school. Yes, she never talked about him. Like, ever. But there was a reason for that. She didn't like to latch on to the past. It did her no favors and usually ended up hurting her more than anything else. She couldn't even remember the last time she saw Levi in the flesh—fine, she'd stalked his Facebook profile a long time ago—so what was the big deal?

"You should mind." Harper leaned in and murmured, "He asked about you."

Her heart started to race. "Really?" She cleared her throat to get rid of the squeak. The pointed look Harper sent her wasn't helping matters. "What did he say?"

"He asked if you still lived here, and I said of course." Harper raised her brows. "Then he said he'd love to see you while he was visiting."

"How long is he visiting?"

"I don't know. I don't really care. And neither should you." Harper grabbed Wren's arm again and gave it a little shake. "Don't forget what he did to you."

"That happened years ago." Wren carefully pulled her arm out of Harper's grip. "I'm over it. You know me. I don't hold grudges."

"When it comes to Levi, maybe you should," Harper muttered.

"I'm not going to hide from him. Just…seat us, and if we happen to see each other, then so be it. If not, no biggie. I'll be fine," Wren said.

With a put-upon sigh, Harper led Wren over to a table. "He's on the other side of the restaurant. Don't say I didn't warn you," Harper said snippily before she strode away.

Wren kept her head bent, flipping open the menu even though she already knew what she would order. She was so tempted to glance over her shoulder, scan the room in search of Levi, but she didn't want him to catch her looking.

So stupid.

Tate slid into the booth within minutes, oblivious to everything that just happened. "Already know what you want to order?"

She closed the menu and lifted her head to smile at him. "Always."

"Good. Me too." The waitress chose that moment to appear by their table, taking their drink and food orders before she snatched up the menus and walked away.

"She usually flirts with me," Tate said once the waitress was gone. "I guess bringing you here just blew any chance I might've had with her." When her smile faded, so did his. "I was kidding. Seriously."

His words, the way he looked at her, sent a shiver down a spine. "Okay," Wren said slowly, though he was probably right. All the women of Wildwood seemed to trip over themselves whenever they were in Tate's presence. Young or old, single or attached. "I think pretty much every woman in this town would give you a second chance. Or a third. Or a fourth…"

"Yeah, yeah. Whatever you say, Dove." He took a packet of sugar out of the container and started to play with it, batting it back and forth across the table between his hands. "Would you ever consider giving me a second chance?"

He almost sounded nervous asking the question. She couldn't help but find that sweet. "I'm pretty sure I've never even given you a real chance yet," she teased, her voice soft. Though she vaguely remembered saying he'd blown his chance with her before…

"Would you? Give me a chance?" He lifted his head, aiming that piercing green gaze right at her, and she blinked, stunned at his words, her heart picking up speed when he said nothing else.

"Are you asking for one?"

Tate smiled and reached across the table, taking her hand in his and entwining their fingers. She shivered at his touch, not even caring if anyone saw the two of them holding hands in the middle of the BFD. She sort of didn't want this moment to end. The entire day had been magical thanks to Tate. "When it comes to you, I'd ask for just about anything."

Wren parted her lips, ready to answer, to tease him a little more, to tell him they should forget the stupid burgers and go back to his place, when a familiar male voice called her name. Her heart in her throat, she slowly turned her head to find Levi Hamilton standing in front of their table.

Oh, crap.

Looking better than ever.

THE DUDE WAS staring at Wren like he had stars in his eyes. Worse, like he was the luckiest damn bastard in the entire universe because he just discovered her. As if she were some sort of foreign land he'd been in search of and dying to conquer for his entire life.

Tate knew that look. Had been experiencing the many confusing emotions behind it for weeks, quietly desperate to claim Wren-land for himself.

"Levi," she breathed, her voice…changing. She never talked to Tate like that, all breathless and light, her tone full of nostalgia and fond memories. "It's—good to see you."

Wren pulled her hand from his and slid out of the booth without any prompting, stepping into the stranger's arms. He was around their age, maybe a little older than Wren but probably younger than Tate, with golden-brown hair cropped close on the sides and longish on top and wearing a pale blue polo shirt and khaki shorts, not one fucking wrinkle in sight.

The asshole could've walked straight out of a Ralph Lauren ad. Tate hated him on sight.

Levi squeezed her tight, his eyes closing for the briefest moment before he released his hold on her. Tate could only sit there gaping at the two of them, trying his best to fight the jealousy churning in his gut.

"How are you?" Levi asked as she slowly pulled away from him, his hands still clinging to her arms. His smile was huge, his eyes only for Wren. "You look amazing. It's been way too long since I've seen you, Wrennie."

Wrennie? What the fuck? Who was this guy?

"I'm great. Well, sort of." She laughed, waved her hands around as if she didn't know what to do with them.

Adorably awkward with her flushed cheeks and helpless expression. "I don't know if you heard…"

"Your house burned down." Levi's expression went solemn, and he reached out to clasp her hand, entwining their fingers. "My parents told me. That's so…awful. I'm sorry that happened to you. What are you going to do? Where are you living?"

"Don't worry about me. I've got it all figured out." She sounded like a liar, even to Tate. She had nothing figured out. Tate knew she was still completely overwhelmed by all that she needed to take care of.

"I do worry about you. I think about you all the time." His gaze briefly flickered to Tate before returning to Wren, completely dismissing him. "I still like to think of me being the guy who was always there for you."

She laughed, the sound nervous and just the slightest bit…irritated? "Right. I figured you forgot all about me once you left town."

"Never." The gentle smile Levi offered Wren made Tate's blood boil.

Anger surged within him. Who was this asshole to tell Wren he'd be there for her? Tate was the one who'd been there for her from the very start. She lived with him. Not this guy who appeared out of nowhere and got to hug her too close and stare at her like he wanted to devour her whole.

Fuck this guy and his supposed good intentions.

Tate was about to stand and tell the guy to fuck off when Wren pulled her hand from Levi's, turning to look at Tate, a nervous smile on her face. "Levi, this is my friend, Tate."

Friend. Nice one, Wrennie.

"Nice to meet you." Tate rose to his feet, noting that he towered over the guy. Good. He thrust out his hand and squeezed Levi's extra hard.

"Likewise." Levi sized him up with a glance, dismissing him when they released hands, and Tate sat back down, his attention all for Wren. Again. "We need to get together before I leave."

"How long are you here for?" she asked as she settled back into the booth across from Tate. Thank Christ. Tate was afraid she might've left with this asshole.

She'd never ditch you.

Tate frowned. He couldn't be too sure of that.

"A few more days. Told my parents we had to stop by the BFD. I haven't been here in what feels like forever." Levi smiled and rocked back on his heels. Jackass acted like he was in no hurry to leave.

Tate stewed, chewing on his lips so he wouldn't snarl and say something rude. Like, *Get the fuck out of here.*

"Hasn't changed much has it?" Wren laughed.

"No, it hasn't. I have good memories of this place." Levi's voice dropped. "I'm sure you remember."

Okay, that was it. Tate squeezed his hands into fists, ready to use them if necessary when, lucky for Levi, the waitress appeared with their drinks. She plunked down Tate's iced tea and Wren's Sprite before she scurried away. The interruption seemed to be just what Levi needed.

"I should get going. But call me, okay? I mean it, Wrennie. We need to catch up. And my parents' number hasn't changed, so I'm sure you remember it. You called it enough times over the years." Levi chuckled, but Wren said nothing. She at least had the decency to appear uncomfortable.

Levi barely looked in Tate's direction. "Nice meeting you," he muttered.

"Same," Tate said tightly.

Levi hesitated, then leaned in and pressed a quick kiss to Wren's cheek before he backed away from the booth. "See ya around, Wrennie."

The moment he was gone, Tate leaned back in his seat, relief making him feel weak. "*Wrennie?* Seriously? And you have the nerve to complain to me about the bird names?"

"Stop. Please. We've known each other forever." Wren's face was flaming red, and she grabbed her Sprite, taking a huge drink. Most likely trying to avoid any more conversation, Tate guessed.

"Who is he anyway?" He was proud of his calm, even voice, like nothing could bother him. Deep down, his stomach was twisted into knots, and his appetite had pretty much evaporated.

He'd really been looking forward to a BFD cheeseburger basket too, damn it.

"Levi's my ex-boyfriend from high school. He graduated a year before I did, and we broke up—it was messy. Stupid. We were young. It was for the best." She shook her head, her cheeks still pink, her eyes…full of longing? Hell, he hoped not. "We haven't seen each other in forever."

"Really." His voice was flat, his stomach twisting harder.

"Really." She glanced toward the entrance, her gaze lingering on the door. What, did she wish she'd left with her high school ex? "He's nothing."

Tate didn't argue. What was the point? She'd just deny whatever he had to say.

But he did know one thing. That Levi asshole didn't look like nothing.

No, he looked more like competition.

Chapter Thirteen

SEXUAL FRUSTRATION RUINED a man's mood like nothing else. Tate was a walking, talking, breathing example of it on this very shitty morning as he made his appearance at the fire station. On his day off, when he could be sleeping in with a fine-looking woman wrapped around him.

Not that any of that particular scenario happened. Damn it.

"What do you know about Levi Hamilton?" Tate tried his best to keep a straight face, not wanting to reveal even a hint of emotion in his voice or expression. If West noticed anything unusual, he'd jump all over it.

And he'd never stop giving Tate shit—one of West's favorite things to do.

West turned to look at him, his eyebrows raised. "Levi Hamilton? Now there's a blast from the past. I haven't seen that guy in years. Pretty much forgot he even existed."

Just the sort of answer Tate wanted to hear. He'd come by the fire station for a scheduled meeting with Josh Bailey, the arson investigator. He was giving them an update on the recent fires—specifically, details on Wren's house. Tate promised he'd let Wren know whatever information he could find out.

"But you do remember him, right?" Tate asked.

"Of course I remember him. Little punk asshole that dated my sister and broke her heart before he left for college." West grimaced. "Levi always did think he was better than the rest of us."

"What do you know about him?" Tate asked, repeating himself but not really caring. Damn it, he wanted more details. Wren wasn't talking. After seeing Levi at the BFD, the mood had shifted for the rest of the day. They went back to his place, watched a movie on Netflix, and went to bed early.

In separate beds.

Yeah. The night had definitely not gone as Tate had planned. The day had started with such promise too. Until she saw Levi and, for whatever reason, he threw a wrench in their unspoken plans, like an invisible third wheel looming in the background of his house.

Tate sort of hated Levi Hamilton.

"Why do you care? Did Wren mention him to you? I haven't heard his name pass her lips since I don't know when. Once he dumped her, she mourned and cried for a little bit, but then she moved on. Wren's always been good at that. Moving on," West explained.

Tate wasn't so sure he liked the sound of that. "I met him yesterday at the BFD. He was there with his parents, visiting I guess."

"Huh. Last I heard he graduated college and moved to Southern California. Orange County, I think. He's some big financer type, makes a lot of money, his major life goal." West sneered. "Was he decked out in designer clothes with a Rolex around his wrist?"

"I don't remember seeing a watch, but his clothes didn't have one wrinkle in them," Tate said, his voice full of disgust.

West chuckled. "Sounds like Levi. He was nice enough when he and my sister were together and happy, but shit. They were just kids. My mom always claimed they weren't right for each other, though she never told Wren that. They weren't in the same league, she said."

"What, like Levi was too good for her?" Tate was offended. Just because the asshole had money didn't mean that he was better than anyone else. Screw that.

"Nah. It was just…Levi's family was wealthy, and we weren't, and it gave Wren an inferiority complex. Our mom hated that. I hated it too. Levi always acted like a smug bastard, like Wren was lucky to have him, you know? When it was more the other way around. That little prick was lucky to have my sister. *She* was the one who was too good for him," West explained.

Exactly what Tate wanted to hear. West's words proved Levi was an asshole, just like he thought. "Thanks for being so forthcoming," he said wryly.

West chuckled and shook his head. "I don't like it when my sister gets hurt. She's the only one I've got. And since she's the lone girl among all of us boys, we're over-protective." The chuckle disappeared and West sent him a meaningful look. "We still are."

Tate got the hint loud and clear. "I'm not out to hurt Wren." He wasn't sure what he was doing with Wren. He'd kissed her once and he wanted more.

Needed more.

"The fact that you took her in when she had nowhere else to go earned you brownie points," West said. "Though if your ulterior motive for this is to get her into your bed, I'll beat your ass."

Like he'd ever tell West that. He wasn't an idiot. "We're friends," Tate stressed. "That's it."

"Well, you better tell her that."

"I don't think she really cares. She's too wrapped up in seeing Levi again," Tate muttered.

"Ah, jealous much? You're not acting much like a friend right now."

Whatever. He was a man who wanted to have sex with his friend. Perfectly normal. That whole just-friends thing was hard to maintain, and he realized quick the more time he spent with Wren, the more he liked her. Lately they'd spent a lot of time together.

Meaning he liked her a hell of a lot.

"If you don't like Levi, then I don't like Levi," Tate said, trying not to sound too defensive. "He seems like an asshole."

"Then he hasn't changed much."

"He wants to see Wren. Hang out with her." *Stare dreamily into her eyes. Kiss her. Strip her naked. Fuck her hard, before he left her again, crying alone in the dust.*

Tate blinked. Where did those thoughts come from? And why did he feel so damn possessive at the mere idea of Wren being with another man? Worse, her first love? There were all sorts of emotions usually tangled up in an old high school romance.

"Barf," West said, making Tate chuckle. Who said *barf* anyway? "I hope she makes up some excuse and doesn't talk to him. Guys like that, they're trouble."

"Why do you say that?" Tate asked.

West shrugged. "Because it's true. He only cares about himself and what he wants or needs. Forget what Wren wants. With Levi, it's all about…Levi."

Tate frowned. He could say the same about himself. He'd wanted to get in Wren's panties for so long it was all he could think about. Now that he'd actually gotten to know the woman and realized how much he enjoyed being with her, he definitely wanted more. He wanted to know more, learn more, discover more. Wren made him feel greedy.

More, more, more.

Those words were a mantra in his head. Unrelenting. Reminding him yet again what hadn't happened last night. She had to know he wanted more though. Right? Or was she clueless? Was she going to run back to that idiot high school ex and try to remake memories?

Hell, he hoped not.

"That's why you shouldn't mess around with her either. You're not good with your feelings," West said, his gruff words interrupting Tate's thoughts.

How the hell did West know he wasn't good with his feelings? And when did he become an authority on another guy's *feelings*? He sounded like a pussy-whipped asshole. Like Harper Hill had West by the balls and refused to ever let them go.

Fucking great.

The idea of falling into that type of situation terrified him. Is that what he had to look forward to if he ever got into a serious relationship? Wren clamping her fingers around his nuts and never letting them go? Hell, making a permanent gesture by forcing him to tattoo her name on his fucking ball sac and proudly proclaiming him as her property?

A shiver moved through him. Yeah, he'd gone off the rails with that last thought, but he couldn't help it. That sort of behavior was exactly why he'd avoided relationships. All the permanency, the mere idea of having one woman for the rest of his life…it was scary stuff.

"You don't know shit about my feelings," Tate muttered, shaking his head.

"Right. Fairly certain we've had this conversation before, and just like last time, it revolves around Wren and your intentions in regards to my sister. I'm hoping you get what I'm saying." West tried to stare him down, but Tate only rolled his eyes. "I'm serious. Don't fuck with her heart, Warren. Or I'll fuck with your—"

A knock sounded, startling them both, their heads jerking toward the open door. Josh paused in the doorway, his expression grim, stride purposeful as he entered the tiny office. He nodded at them in greeting before he settled into the chair next to Tate's. "Good morning, ladies," he murmured, taking a sip of the coffee he clutched in his hand before he spoke again. "Hope I'm not disturbing you two lovebirds."

Tate wanted to roll his eyes but controlled himself. The guy could actually have some solid, interesting information, and trying to find the crafty arsonist was driving them all crazy. They were like stupid puppies chasing their tails but never able to catch them. Whoever the son of a bitch was, he strung them along, too damn smart for his own good. Scary smart.

He hated it. They all hated it, especially Josh. Oh, and Lane Gallagher. The arsonist got Lane's cop blood pumping, but the investigation wasn't under his jurisdiction, and that infuriated him. Not that Tate could blame him.

"What's going on?" West asked, getting right to the point. "Who burned my sister's house down?"

Josh held out his hand in a defensive gesture, shaking his head once. "We don't know yet. The incident is still under investigation." He took a deep breath, glancing at Tate quickly. As if he knew what he was about to say would piss him off. "I can't rule out yet that the fire wasn't started by the occupant."

"Are you saying *Wren* started the fire? You gotta be fucking kidding me," Tate all but roared. West sent him a look, and he clamped his lips shut, trying to contain his fury, but it was no use. The words burst from him like he had no control. "Why the hell would she do that anyway? She lost *everything*. Every single thing she owned with the exception of the clothes on her back and a few things she'd left in her car. She doesn't even have renter's insurance."

"I'm not saying she set it on purpose," Josh said, his voice calm and quiet. Which only infuriated Tate even more. He wanted to punch Josh in his smug-looking face. "It was most likely an accident."

"No." Tate shook his head. "I refuse to believe it." He crossed his arms in front of his chest. Bailey had a lot of nerve, accusing Wren of setting her own place on fire. She wasn't even home when the fire started. How the hell could she have done it?

Leaving a curling iron on, or whatever the hell women used to primp and make themselves pretty. Or maybe she forgot to blow out a candle that burned for so many hours, the flame became higher…eventually catching a curtain on fire.

Tate frowned. He didn't like thinking along those lines. Blaming her. She was smart. She came from a family of firefighters and he knew she wasn't careless. She'd never leave a candle burning or a curling iron plugged in. She wasn't stupid.

But sometimes we all do stupid things. You know this. You're an expert at making dumb moves. Look at how you're letting Wren slip right through your fingers and back into the arms of her arrogant ex.

Tate shoved the negative thoughts into the farthest corner of his brain.

"I'm not ruling it out yet," Josh said carefully. "But we'll see."

"That's all you've got?" West asked incredulously.

Josh's expression betrayed nothing. The guy was one serious nut who proved almost impossible to crack. "That's all I'm willing to discuss regarding the fire at Wren Gallagher's residence. Otherwise, we have no new leads, no new fires. The Ridge fire has officially been declared as arson—"

"We already knew that," Tate interrupted, earning a hard stare from Josh for doing so.

"Right. And that's it."

"Why the hell did you call this meeting then?" West asked.

"I wanted to let you both know that I'm not quite sure if Wren's house was set by the arsonist. See if you have any info in regards to the fire or to…Wren's state of mind over the last few weeks, especially before the incident happened," Josh said.

"How are we supposed to know?" West made a face.

Inside, Tate seethed. He knew what Josh was getting at. And it pissed him off.

"Was she upset? Was something bothering her? Distracting her?" Josh looked from West to Tate, his gaze sticking to Tate. "Relationship troubles possibly?"

"Are you implying something?" Tate asked tightly.

"Not at all. You two are the closest to her, from what I can tell. Well, and your brother Lane. But that guy would rather pummel me into the ground than give me the time of day," Josh muttered with a shake of his head.

Tate could relate. Lane was a solid judge of character.

"Well, our mother was going through some health problems…" West's voice drifted, and Tate sent him a meaningful look. One that said shut the fuck up.

West pressed his lips together, remaining quiet.

"She didn't do it," Tate said after a few moments of tense silence. "I know Wren. I've spent a lot of time with her lately, and I know she wouldn't do something as careless as you're implying. I don't care how supposedly distracted or worried she might've been. She knows better."

"I'm glad you have so much faith in her." Josh stood. "She's going to need someone standing by her side."

The moment Josh walked out of the office, West cursed under his breath. "I really dislike that guy."

"You and me both," Tate muttered.

"THANK YOU FOR agreeing to meet with me." Levi smiled at her, revealing his perfectly white, perfectly straight teeth. She remembered back in high school when he wore braces. Remembered when he used to flip his hair away from his eyes with a flick of his head, a gesture she always found incredibly cute. The way his brown eyes would crinkle in the corners every time he looked at her and smiled.

They were crinkling now as he watched her from across the table at the tiny local coffee shop tourists loved to come to. The end of the season was close, but there were still people flooding the area. Labor Day weekend was the final close-out for the summer, and it loomed.

It still surprised her that Levi was in Wildwood visiting his parents. It shouldn't, considering his family never left. But if he came back over the years, she'd never heard about it. Though what gave her the right to know? After he ended their relationship, they didn't even remain friends.

But just maybe…they *could* change that and become friends after all. She definitely didn't want anything more. They were long done. Surely he had a girlfriend or even a…wife.

Her gaze dropped to his hands resting loosely on the tiny round table, and she leaned in closer, trying to see if he had a wedding ring on.

"So tell me. What's up with you? What's been going on for the last nine years?" he asked, drawing her attention back to his face. Staring into his warm brown eyes brought back a flood of memories, the majority of them pleasant. It was weird, how he felt so familiar yet like a stranger too.

How could she catch him up on nine years in only a few minutes? Ugh, she was a talker. It was both her greatest asset and biggest fault. Her incessant chatter had always driven her family crazy, but Levi never seemed to mind.

Then he dumped her, and she'd been so sad, yet so pissed, all at once. Why she was even talking to him, she wasn't sure.

"There's not much to tell. I never left Wildwood, so how exciting could my life be?" Before he could protest, she continued, "You already know about the biggest thing that happened to me this summer. My entire life just went up in smoke. Poof." She laughed, trying to make light of the fire, but when she saw the sympathy flare in his gaze, she knew she blew it. Houses burning to the ground weren't that funny.

"So awful, Wrennie," he murmured with a shake of his head. "Do they think it's the arsonist?" His voice was laced with concern. Hearing him mention the arsonist set her back a bit. Being a part of the firefighting community, she'd always known things before anyone else did. Not that any confidentialities were broken, but the Gallagher family always seemed to have the inside track when it came to local fire or police information. "My parents mentioned there have been a lot of fires here this summer," he explained, no doubt because of the surprised expression on her face.

"I don't know exactly what's going on with the investigation, but I believe arson is suspected," she answered carefully. She didn't want to reveal too much information, not that she knew anything.

"Terrible. I can't imagine what you've suffered because of this."

"It hasn't been so bad," she started, but he shook his head, cutting her off.

"Next thing you know the entire town is on fire. Why isn't anyone doing anything about this?" He sounded angry.

She laughed, though it was forced. "I think they'll find him before anything as drastic as all of Wildwood burning happens." Her brothers wouldn't allow it. Neither would Tate.

Her heart ached just thinking of him. She knew he was frustrated. She'd been so distracted after they ran into Levi at the BFD, the entire rest of the evening had been ruined. She'd felt guilty about that.

So guilty.

"Who says it's a him?" Levi raised his brows, reaching for his iced vanilla latte and taking a sip. "It could be a woman too."

"Doubtful. Most arsonists are male." She could recite a list of facts on arsonists she'd learned from her father over the years, but she didn't want to bore him with those details. "Now come on. You don't want to hear my entire sob story. It's boring. Tell me what's new with you."

He glanced down at the table and smiled, looking downright…bashful? That was so un-Levi of him. "There's not much to tell."

Wren grabbed her cup and sipped from her white chocolate iced mocha. Maybe they hadn't spoken or seen each other in years, but she knew Levi loved to go on about himself. He'd always had a big ego and needed it stroked. She'd accommodated him, thinking that was what good girlfriends did.

Now she knew better. This time she was just digging for information to see what he'd been up to since he left.

"Come on. We haven't talked in forever," she coaxed, making his smile grow. "Have you even been back to Wildwood since you left for college?"

"Of course I have." He looked downright offended at her question. "Always brief visits though. Work never allows me to get away for too long. Sometimes my parents come to visit me."

"Where are you living now? Last I heard you were in Los Angeles." Why did she just say that? He probably thought she was keeping tabs on him.

But it was like he didn't even notice what she said. "I live in San Francisco. I, uh…well, you wouldn't believe what happened, but I created this app with a friend, and it sort of took off." Levi launched into a description of the app, how it revolved around banking and keeping track of various accounts and investments. The longer he talked, the more bored she got, folding her straw wrapper into a tiny accordion, stretching it out between her fingers before smushing it back in.

He said something about how he used to live in Los Angeles before moving to San Francisco almost two years ago, since that's where all the app designers lived, and how he bought a house in the same neighborhood as Mark Zuckerberg.

That little tidbit made her ears perk right up.

"Wait a minute. You live in the same neighborhood as Zuckerberg? Founder of Facebook?"

"I do." He smiled. "It's in the Mission District. Great house, completely renovated with all the modern necessities while keeping the exterior true to its original look. The place is three stories and with a fantastic view of the bay."

Levi was so enthusiastic about his house and his job, and that was great, but his words also felt like he was…showing off? But she shouldn't think that way. He had reason to be proud. She'd be proud too if she created a popular app and lived in the same neighborhood as the creator of Facebook.

"Sounds nice." She smiled at him, going for polite, yet hating the nagging feeling that churned inside her. Since when had her first love been so boring?

"Yeah, that's one way to put it. I think you'd love my house, and the neighborhood. I know how you've always loved San Francisco." His smile faded, his expression going super serious in a frightening short amount of time. "You should come visit."

She was touched that he remembered her love of the city, but no way could she go visit him. "Oh, I don't think—"

"I mean it," he interrupted. "I'd love for you to come see me, Wren. I have plenty of room." He reached across the table and took her hand. She let him, curious to see if she'd experience that same old rush of tingles sweeping up her arm at his touch.

It was...pleasant. His hand was soft, not rough with calluses. Not like a man who worked with his hands. But his fingers were long, his palm wide. His touch comforted, and that was...

Pleasant.

Wait a minute. You already thought that particular word.

"Can I make a confession?"

His soft question accompanied by the equally soft smile curving his mouth temporarily rendered her mute. She could only nod in reply.

"It was...strange, seeing you at first," he said as he squeezed her hand in his. "It's been so long, and you've changed so much."

Wren frowned. She had? Really?

"Yet you also look exactly the same. It's crazy. And I mean that in a good way. Seeing you after all these years, all of those old memories came back." He hesitated, tilting his head to the side so their gazes met. "And there were a lot of good times for us, right, Wrennie?"

She nodded, remaining silent, hating how he called her Wrennie. It sounded so stupid and immature—and incredibly intimate when they hadn't shared any intimate moments in years. She didn't feel close to him, not like that. And she wasn't that girl anymore either. Though yes, she could admit there were a lot of good memories between them, there were some bad ones too. Like the big one, when he dumped her out of nowhere, leaving her a heartbroken seventeen-year-old while he ran off to college and partied into oblivion. She could only imagine the drunken escapades he got himself into. The parties, the drinking, the new friends he made, the girls.

All the many girls he banged.

Her teenage heart could hardly bear the thought.

"Talking to you reminded me of all those good times we shared. I realized then how much I missed having you in my life." He interlaced their fingers together, the hand-holding turning intimate with one simple movement. "I know we can't pick up where we left off. Too much time and too many things have happened since then, and we've both changed so much. I'm curious though. Would you ever considering giving me a…second chance?"

Wren blinked at him, her brain almost sluggish as it tried to compute his words. Was he for real? Did he just ask her for a second chance? After all this time? He'd left her and never looked back. Never bothered calling her, writing her a letter, an email, a text...nothing. Just up and left for college and continued living his life like she never existed. Once he was gone, she rarely saw his parents around town either. It was like the entirety of the Hamiltons had faded from her life once he broke it off.

And now he waltzed right back into town like he never left it. Flashed her a smile and held her hand while recounting those fond old memories, only to hit her with a, *Hey, let's try this again?*

Um, no thanks.

"I'm flattered you would ask for a second chance," she murmured, trying to tug her hand out of his, but he wouldn't let go. "I think it's great and all, that we have this shared history."

"It's a solid foundation to build a true and lasting relationship on," he explained, his gaze gentle, his smile sweet.

"Right." She nodded. He sounded so...sincere. Yet not. It was strange. This entire moment had just turned strange, and she hoped like crazy she could get herself out of it without inflicting any damage. Even after all this time, she still didn't want to hurt him. Ridiculous. "But I think too much time has passed between us, Levi. We can't try to get back what we used to share. It's gone. There's nothing we can do about it."

She didn't want to do anything about it. She was circling around Tate, and he was circling around her. He liked her despite her snarky defense mechanism and that she could beat him at swimming. She liked him too.

She planned on telling him that she met with Levi the moment she got home. No secrets between them. She needed to be open and honest.

Tate deserved to know the truth.

His gaze was steady, his voice so deep and serious as he spoke. "Do you really believe that, Wrennie?"

"Please don't call me Wrennie." Ugh. He looked hurt over her saying that, but she couldn't let this go on. "And I do believe that. Let's leave our relationship where it was— in the past. And let's focus on being friends now. That will be much easier." She didn't want to try again with Levi. He didn't deserve a second chance. Yeah, maybe they could be friends, but they could never share such intimate moments together ever again. That ship between them had long since sailed, and she couldn't imagine Levi as her boyfriend ever again.

But clearly he could. And he liked the idea too.

"You don't have a girlfriend?" she asked, trying her best to keep her voice even. She didn't want him to get the wrong idea. She was asking because she was curious, not because she wanted to pursue something with him.

"We split up a few months ago," he admitted, hanging his head briefly before lifting it, his gaze meeting hers. "She got the dog in the divorce."

"You were married?" She was shocked, though she probably shouldn't be. Enough years had passed that he could've gotten married and divorced.

He laughed and shook his head. "Nah. Never married. We did live together, but we split about six months ago. She took the dog, claiming I was never home so I didn't deserve to keep him. I loved that damn dog. Pretty coldhearted, how she took him away from me, don't you think?"

Wren once again said nothing. They'd split only six months ago, meaning she was most likely a rebound consideration. And she deserved more than that.

"I'm ready for something serious. Something meaningful. Once Linda and I split, I kept thinking about...you. I Googled you." He at least looked contrite with the admission. "I was curious. You never looked me up online?"

"No." She shook her head. His disappointment was obvious, reminding her of what an egomaniac Levi had always been. It was always me, me, me. The world revolved around him.

"Well, I'm hoping you would've been pleasantly surprised. And proud of me. I've accomplished a lot so far, and I'm just getting started." He smiled, rather pleased with himself. "I'm a catch, Wren. I can't lie. But I don't want anyone else. I want you. I can take care of you. Give you a home. We can live in the city. You always did love San Francisco. Remember when my parents took us there that one time?"

She did remember. More, she was the tiniest bit touched he remembered her love for the city. How she dreamed of living there when she grew up. Well, she was all grown up and still stuck in the same small town while he was almost...what?

Living her dream? No, more like living her teenaged self's dream.

Her head wasn't in the clouds anymore. She was firmly rooted in reality. And her reality didn't involve Levi.

"I was a jerk when I broke up with you. I realized that right away but didn't know how to tell you. I was young and stupid, and I was afraid you hated me." His gaze pleaded, his expression earnest. "Tell me you don't hate me. Please."

"I don't hate you." The words were honest. How could she hate him? She wasn't the type to hold a grudge. But too much had happened, too many years had passed.

He watched her like he expected her to say something, but what? Her mind drew a blank. She needed to let him down easy. Needed to tell him she wasn't interested.

But the words never came.

Chapter Fourteen

WREN STILL HADN'T come home, and it was late. Way past dinnertime, when she told him she'd be back. This was his last night off before he went back on shift, and though he hadn't told her, he was hoping they could spend it together. Doing whatever she wanted, preferably naked.

And in his bed.

That she still wasn't here and it was creeping up on nine o'clock was his own damn fault. He could've told her he wanted to see her, but he hadn't wanted to look too needy.

Tate scrubbed his hand over his face. *Christ.* The girl was making him feel needy. Like a lovesick idiot.

He prowled around his house. Unloaded the dishwasher. Folded and put away his laundry. Performed all the usual mundane tasks he normally did the night before he went back to work. But throughout it all, he felt different. Lonely. He missed having Wren around. He'd always been a solitary creature before. Living alone suited him just fine. He dealt with enough people at work when he was stuck at the station for four days straight, sometimes longer when he was working overtime.

Going home was his quiet time. His sanctuary. But having Wren around, knowing she was at his house even when he wasn't there, he…liked it.

Wasn't sure what to do about it either.

It was almost eleven before he finally heard the dead bolt turn and the front door open and close quietly from within his bedroom. He'd left only a single lamp on in the living room. The rest of the house was dark, and she probably thought he was asleep. He should just let her go to her own room and forget about tonight. It was none of his business, asking where she was. Or whom she was with. The sneaking suspicion that had lingered all night clawed at him, forced him to go to his bedroom door and push it open.

Wren was tiptoeing down the hall with sandals dangling from her fingers. She came to a stop when she saw him, her eyes wide, shoulders going back as she stood straighter, a guilty expression on her face. His gaze swept over her, taking every little detail in. The pale pink sundress she wore with the slightly flared skirt that hit her just above the knees bared plenty of skin and hugged her curves. His skin went hot, and his dick twitched, yet he hadn't even touched her. Hell, he couldn't take his eyes off her. She looked so fresh and pretty, her hair pulled up into a high ponytail and exposing that elegant neck he wanted to feast on with his lips and tongue. Her cheeks were rosy and her eyes wide, like she was embarrassed he caught her sneaking into the house.

"I thought you were sleeping," she said softly.

"I was worried about you," he admitted as he leaned against the doorframe, crossing his arms in front of his chest. Her gaze dropped to his arms, her eyes warming appreciatively, and a surge of lust shot through him. If she wanted him so damn bad, why hadn't she come home sooner? Why had she taken off at all? When did everything get so fucked up and confusing?

The next words came out of his mouth as if he had no control over them. "You said you'd be home for dinner." He sounded like a nagging wife.

She winced and took a step backward. "I'm so sorry. You didn't make us dinner, did you?"

"No, you're off the hook for that. You don't need to apologize." She looked relieved, but he didn't want her relieved. He wanted her to realize he'd been waiting for her. He wanted to know where the hell she'd been.

More like who the hell she had been *with*.

"Okay, good. I'll make it up to you." Her face brightened, and she smiled. "I'll make you dinner tomorrow."

"I go back to work tomorrow."

The light dimmed in her eyes, and she propped her shoulder against the wall. "Oh. Right. Maybe another time then."

Tate waited for her to admit where she'd been, but she remained quiet. The way she dipped her head told him she wouldn't necessarily look him in the eye either.

Confirmation that she'd been with exactly whom he thought.

"You were with your ex." He didn't phrase it as a question. He knew she'd been with Levi Hamilton. Damn it, he didn't even know the guy, but he hated him.

She lifted her head, the shoes she'd clutched dropping to the floor with a soft clatter. Shock etched across her features as she folded her arms in front of her chest, plumping up her breasts. Yeah, he noticed. Even when he was frustrated with her he couldn't help but check out her tits. "You're right, I was with him earlier. We, uh, went to coffee and played catch-up. Then I went over to Delilah's and hung out for a little bit."

"Did you have a good time strolling down memory lane?" He sounded like a jealous asshole, which was accurate because he *felt* like a jealous asshole, something he hadn't experienced since when? High school? That he was jealous over some punk dick who strutted back into town and messed with his ex-girlfriend's head all for his own selfish needs infuriated him.

"It was…" She hesitated, as if searching for the right words. "Weird. And confusing."

Not the answer he expected. "Why?"

Wren curled her arms tighter around her middle. "Levi said some things that…surprised me."

Tate didn't want to pull it out of her, but she wasn't being particularly forthcoming either. If he kept badgering her, it would seem like he cared, and she might misinterpret his questioning.

But if he was being honest with himself, he *did* care. He cared a lot. Never had he felt this way about a woman before, especially a woman with whom he had a platonic relationship. Yeah, they'd flirted. A lot. He'd felt her up in his bed. Had his mouth on her skin. Kissed her just once. But he still didn't know what she looked like when she came. Or what his name falling from her lips as she moaned sounded like.

He wanted to know all of those things and a million more when it came to Wren. She held herself back with him, much like he did with everyone. Keeping people at a distance meant they couldn't really know him.

Wren though. She was a mystery he desperately wanted to figure out.

"I'd bore you with all the details. Nothing's going on with me and Levi. Trust me." She dropped her arms and pushed away from the wall with a weary smile. "Besides, I already unloaded enough on Delilah. I should probably let you get your sleep. Good night, Tate."

She was about to turn and walk into her temporary bedroom when he stepped forward, wrapping his fingers around her upper arm. Pausing, she turned to look at him over her shoulder, her eyes wide, her full lips parted. Her tongue darted out, and she licked at the corner of her mouth, her expression nothing short of nervous and, fuck, still so sexy. He didn't want her unsure and timid around him. Screw that.

"You can unload on me anytime," he said, careful to keep his voice even and meaning every word. "Whatever's bothering you, if you need to talk, I'm here for you. Even if I'm the one who's bothering you."

"Well. You do drive me crazy sometimes." Her smile returned, faintly tipping up the corners of her mouth. God, he couldn't stop staring at her fucking lips. He wanted them. Wanted to taste and tease, nip and lick and suck.

"I thought so." He loosened his hold on her arm, skimming his thumb across her skin in a gentle caress. Goose bumps formed, and the tiniest shiver moved through her. "Do you realize I haven't even really *kissed* you yet? Why? What the hell is wrong with us?"

She gaped at him. Yeah, Wren needed to know he had zero plans on giving up. He wasn't even close to being finished with her. What if that asshole Hamilton was trying to get her back? Fuck that. The jackass needed to go back to the big city where he belonged and leave Wren alone.

Leave Wren for *him*.

"You kissed me at the lake."

"One kiss is not enough," he murmured.

"Oh. You're, um, probably right." Her voice was shaky, her gaze dropping to his lips. As if she wanted them on hers. He stepped closer, his body brushing against hers, forcing her to flatten herself against the wall. Her hair and her skirt rustled with the movement, and her breasts rose and fell with each hurried breath. All he could hear was the sound of their accelerated breathing in the otherwise quiet of the house, the tick of the clock that hung in his kitchen. He slid his hand down her bare arm, his fingers ghosting along her skin. "We should probably try it again. You know, see if we're compatible," she whispered.

"I'm fairly certain we're beyond compatible," he murmured, touching her face, his fingers drifting over her cheek, thumb streaking across her plump lower lip. Her lids fluttered, a gust of warm air caressing his hand, and he leaned in, pressing his forehead against hers. "I missed you tonight, Dove."

She closed her eyes and inhaled deeply, allowing his gaze to zero in on her chest, the hint of cleavage exposed. The top of her dress dipped just low enough to tease, and his mouth watered at all that pretty, smooth skin on display. "You should've texted me."

"I thought you were coming home earlier." He touched her neck, slid his index finger down, down, until he was tracing the neckline of her dress, touching the spot where skin met material. "My feelings for you confuse the hell out of me."

He lifted his gaze and studied her face, the way her delicate brows drew down at his admission, her tongue sneaking out for another quick lick. Lord help him, the woman was driving him crazy.

"I don't want to come on too strong," he confessed when she still hadn't said anything. "But I'm not going to let you slip through my fingers either."

Her eyes opened slowly, her slightly dazed blue eyes staring into his. "You've never shown much restraint around me until now."

Chuckling, he dipped his finger beneath the dress's neckline, touching warm, soft skin, the snug valley between her breasts. She sucked in a harsh breath, goose bumps chasing after his touch. "Suddenly feels like every-thing's on the line, you know?"

"Really?" She sounded surprised. Didn't she see? He wanted her. He'd never done anything like this before, but if he had to fight for her then…he would.

The realization was startling. He'd never had to fight for a woman. Ever.

Tate dropped his hand and shifted even closer to Wren, so their legs tangled and their chests were pressed together. He slipped one arm around her waist, the other hand moving back up to cradle the side of her face as he tilted her head back. Her gaze met his, wide and unblinking. "Before, it was just playing around. I was attracted to you. Wanted to get you in my bed." He dipped his head so his mouth hovered just above hers. "But now all I can think about is, how can I *keep* you in my bed? In my house? In my life?"

Before she could utter a single word, he settled his mouth on hers.

WREN'S HEAD SWAM at the first touch of Tate's warm, damp lips on hers. They moved over hers slowly, as if he were savoring her, savoring this particular moment—their first real kiss. Helplessly she reached out, her fingers catching at the front of his shirt, pulling him closer. He went willingly, his arm tightening around her waist, his other hand sliding from her cheek up into her hair at the exact moment he deepened the kiss. She parted her lips, letting him in. A whimper sounded in her throat when his tongue thoroughly swept her mouth.

He said he wanted to keep her. That he wanted *her*. Evidence of his want pressed against her belly, reminding her that all she had to say was yes.

And he'd be inside her. No questions asked.

She slipped her arms around his neck and buried her hands in his soft hair, a whimper leaving her when he broke the kiss to slide his mouth down the length of her neck. His hot lips blazed a trail along her skin, leaving her weak. Restless.

Terrified.

Could she really have something serious with Tate? She was tempted. So tempted. But what if he hurt her? What if she wasn't good enough? What if he got bored? She was scared. Relationships in general scared her. She didn't want to get hurt. It was easier to pretend you didn't need someone than lay your feelings, all your hopes and dreams, on the line.

Kissing Tate, falling into bed with him, wasn't going to solve her problems—only temporarily, if at all.

Maybe she needed a temporary fix.

"Hey." He broke the kiss, his lips moving against hers when he spoke. "You're not with me."

Blinking her eyes open, she stared up at him, his face so close she could see the myriad colors in his eyes. They weren't solid green, but a mixture of shades of light and dark green, gold, and brown. "I'm with you," she said breathlessly, reaching up to touch the side of his face. His skin was prickly with stubble, and she had the sudden image of all that stubble rubbing against her thighs as he dived between her legs.

Her panties dampened at the mere thought.

"Really." He kissed her nose. "I find it hard." He kissed her cheek. "To believe you." He kissed her other cheek. "Don't tell me you're thinking about him."

Wren's eyes widened. What? She wasn't thinking about Levi. She was worried about herself and the predicament she was in. All of the problems overwhelming her, along with her confusing feelings for Tate. Did he feel the same way? Could he?

"Are you?" Tate repeated, his voice firm. Maybe even a little bit angry. "Are you really kissing me and thinking about your ex?"

"I...no." She shook her head, unsure of what to say next. She'd never been in this kind of situation before, with two men vying for her attention. She'd always thought that could be kind of fun. Such heady stuff, two men wanting her at the same time. What girl wouldn't want to experience that at least once?

But it wasn't fun. Not at all. No, more like it was confusing and terrifying. She didn't want to hurt anyone's feelings. She didn't want to feel like this. And she definitely didn't want to make Tate angry.

But angry, frustrated Tate was pretty hot. His jaw had gone hard, muscle clenching, and his cheeks were ruddy. She'd caught glimpses of that cute dimple in his left cheek quite a bit when he was flirting with her, but all traces of it were gone at this moment. His eyes were dark and full of fire, his brows lowered, his mouth still damp and swollen from their kisses...

Okay, that was really hot. She could literally feel his fingers flex and curl into a fist at the small of her back, like he wanted to punch Levi, which was crazy. She didn't want them to get into a *fight* over her.

Though the idea of two men fighting over her was sort of hot.

"I want to make you forget that guy ever existed." Tate slipped his hand beneath her chin, his thumb and index finger curling around it as he tilted her head back so their gazes met, his turbulent and swirling with anger. "I want to fuck every memory of him right out of you."

She sucked in a sharp breath, and her knees went weak. Should she be offended? Tell him to go to hell? Probably, though truthfully his words only aroused her more, and a helpless little sound escaped her.

His eyes darkened as he skimmed his thumb across her mouth, making it tingle. She parted her lips, about to say something, but he slipped his thumb between her lips, and she darted out her tongue, licking his flesh. His eyes darkened even more, and he removed his thumb from her lips, replacing it with his mouth.

Kissing her until she thought she might drown.

She clutched at him, her hands slipping beneath his T-shirt at the exact moment his fingers gathered up the skirt of her dress. Cool air wafted across her backside when he exposed her, and then his hands were there. Big and warm, sliding over her ass, toying with the pitifully thin fabric of her panties before he dipped his fingers beneath the waistband, touching her bare, sensitive skin.

All the while his mouth consumed. Devoured. He had her pressed to the wall, his hard body flush against hers, his hips grinding, his hands kneading, his tongue thrusting. She whimpered as she jerked his T-shirt up, her hands exploring the hot, wide expanse of his chest. Counting the ridge of muscles in his abdomen, sliding over his pecs, teasing the small patch of hair that grew in the center.

He was all man. Muscled and hot and rough, his hands roaming all over her like he was mapping her skin with his fingers. He kissed like he wanted to possess her, like he already owned her, and when he pushed at her panties with a firm shove, she let him, wiggling her hips so they fell to her thighs.

Breaking the kiss, he knelt before her, his splayed hands gripping her hips. She reached out, bracing her hands on his broad shoulders, her entire body trembling in anticipation of what he would do to her next.

And he didn't disappoint, his head disappearing beneath her dress, his warm, wet mouth on her quivering stomach. She released her hold on him and sagged against the wall, a low moan escaping when he nipped and licked around her belly button, his hand shoving her panties the rest of the way down until they landed around her ankles. She kicked them off, watching in fascination as his head moved beneath her pink skirt, his mouth on her skin, his fingers…

Oh God…his fingers crept up the inside of her thigh. Light, teasing touches as he continued to kiss her belly. It was strangely erotic, seeing his head move under her skirt, feeling his mouth on her skin, his fingers, never really knowing where he would be next.

A low growl escaped him at the precise moment he touched the wet flesh between her legs. She gasped, her entire body going still, eyes falling shut when he stroked her. Back and forth, searching and then finding her clit within seconds, circling it in maddeningly slow circles.

She splayed her hands against the wall, trying to grab hold of something. Anything so she wouldn't slide to the floor. He continued stroking her, one hand lightly gripping her hip, the other between her thighs. She spread her legs wider, the sound of her panting breaths filling the air, accompanied by Tate's fingers caressing her slick flesh. He suddenly ducked his head out from underneath her skirt, and she opened her eyes to find him watching her.

All the air left her lungs as they stared at each other. His hand stilled, his fingers hovering over her sensitive flesh, and she shifted her hips. Lifted them as subtly as she could, hoping he'd get the message and continue what he was doing.

But he didn't move, just kept staring at her. Like he was waiting for her to say something.

"You want to come?" he finally asked, the deep tenor of his voice reaching right into her and making her tremble.

She nodded, her throat as dry as sandpaper, making it impossible to speak.

"Say it, Dove. Tell me you want to come." He touched her clit, a feather-light stroke that made her whimper. The bones in her legs went liquid, and she could feel herself slipping. Her knees buckled, but Tate held her firm, his fingers gripping her hip, his other hand sliding down the inside of her thigh. "I got you, baby. Tell me what you want."

Wren shook her head. She couldn't just ask for it, could she? No man had ever made her say it out loud before. Most of the men she'd been with were sexually proficient and pretty much could always get her there, but she'd gone through a serious dry spell lately. Reading romance novels on her iPad mini and occasionally putting her vibrator to work helped, but there was nothing like a real man's hands. His mouth and tongue on her skin, his gaze devouring her like she was the sexiest thing he'd ever seen.

"Talk to me." His voice was soft, his touch equally so as he pushed the skirt of her dress up, over her hips so that it bunched at her waist. He dipped his head, his mouth grazing her right hip bone, making her shiver. "I won't give you what you want unless you say it."

Oh God, he was playing dirty.

And she liked it.

Chapter Fifteen

"PLEASE," WREN FINALLY managed to squeak out, her eyes sliding shut as she turned her head to the side and pressed her cheek against the cool wall. His hands skimmed up and down her thighs, never touching her exactly where she wanted him, and she almost screamed in frustration.

She was so damn close, hovering on that delicious edge of orgasmic oblivion. She wanted to tumble right over it, fall into the climax she just knew would be amazing. That he could bring her so close in such a short time was like a miracle. Either the man was extremely skilled or she was beyond primed for this.

Probably more like a combination of both.

"Please what?" Tate pressed an openmouthed kiss to the inside of her thigh, so close to the spot where she wanted him. What started out as passionate kissing went from reckless to beyond intimate in a matter of minutes.

"I want to hear you ask for it, Dove. I liked the please bit, but I need more."

He was evil. Sexy and evil and devastatingly handsome. When she said nothing, he flashed her a smile full of dimples, his eyes hooded and dark and full of delicious, tantalizing secrets. She parted her lips, trying to work up the courage to tell him what she wanted, when he touched his mouth to her skin once again. Higher this time, close to the crease where her thigh met her pelvis.

"I can smell you," he whispered, and she whimpered, which only made him smile more. "You're so wet for me, Wren."

"Oh God, make me come, Tate." The words burst from her throat, startling her. "Please."

The smile faded, his eyes grew heated, and he leaned in once more, his mouth brushing her flesh. "With my mouth or my fingers?"

"Both. Both, please."

She closed her eyes and sighed with exquisite relief when his mouth pressed there, exactly where she wanted it. His fingers slipped over wet flesh, two pushing inside as his lips worked her, sucking her clit. She braced her knees, cracking her eyes open so she could watch his dark head move between her legs, and that was when the dam broke.

Shudders swept over her as the orgasm hit her hard, making her cry out. He continued his ministrations, his fingers plunging deep, tongue swirling around her clit, his other hand grasping her hip. She trembled and shook as wave after wave swept over her, tugging her under, making her mind go blank. She could focus only on him, the rhythm of his fingers, the pull of his lips, the flick of his tongue.

Her hips bucked against him, and he pulled his face away from her, his fingers still buried inside her body, his lips shiny. Their gazes met, locked, and she watched in mute fascination as he licked his lips as if he savored the very taste of her. Slowly, without a word, he rose to his feet until he towered over her. His hand curled around her nape, and he lowered his head, his mouth brushing hers. She could taste herself, but it didn't bother her. She deepened the kiss, their tongues tangling, his other arm coming around her and pulling her away from the wall.

"My bed," he growled against her lips. "Now."

Wren let him walk her backward into his bedroom, trusting that he wouldn't steer her wrong. He pulled her dress up and over her head, tossing it on the floor. His eyes heated when he caught sight of her breasts—she wore no bra. She thrust her chest out, thrilled at his perusal. She stood in front of him completely naked while he was still fully dressed.

Courage filling her, she told him, "Sit on the bed."

He did as she asked, his legs spread wide in that way men had, his erection thrusting against the front of his black basketball shorts. Slowly she approached, letting him look his fill, and oh, how he did. His gaze seemed to bounce everywhere, from her face to her breasts to her stomach to her legs. Smiling, she swung her leg over both of his and straddled him, her hands on his shoulders, her breasts in his face. His thighs were hard and thick with muscle, and before she could settle her butt on them, his hands were there, clutching her cheeks, pulling her so close she sucked in a breath.

"You're trying to drive me crazy," he muttered against her chest before he nuzzled her breasts with his face. The stubble on his cheeks abraded her skin, her nipples, and she wrapped her hand around the back of his head, pulling him into her chest.

"Keep doing that," she said, proud that she was able to ask. Demand. Whatever he wanted to call it.

Tate chuckled, the huff of warm breath tickling her skin. "Fuck, you feel so good," he whispered just before he drew a nipple into his mouth and sucked.

She tipped her head back, every pull of his mouth on her nipple sending sparks of pleasure through her veins. He lavished attention on her other breast, nipping and licking her skin, sucking her nipple, trailing his tongue in the valley between her breasts. His hands were still on her backside, pulling her close, closer, until she was rubbing against the hard ridge beneath his shorts, up and down, working herself closer to her second orgasm of the night.

"Could I make you come like this?" he asked, his voice a husky murmur against her skin.

She gazed down at him, running her fingers through his thick, soft hair. "Probably."

He grinned, though it faded quickly when she ground herself against his cock. "Fuck, keep that up and you're going to make *me* come," he said with a groan.

The laugh that escaped surprised her, and she circled her hips again, slower this time, her fingers tightening in his hair. His eyes slid closed, and he made a satisfied noise low in his throat, his hands moving to her hips as he lifted her up and suddenly tossed her on the bed.

And then he was on top of her, shedding his shirt before his mouth attached to hers. She kissed him back with equal enthusiasm, her hands at the waistband of his shorts, shoving them down. Until he was gloriously naked, his skin pressed against hers.

It all happened too fast yet not fast enough. Hands wandered; mouths connected and came apart, exploring those secret spots no one else knows. He kissed her just beneath her breast, making her shiver. She kissed him along his ribs, making him tremble. Somehow he found a condom, and somehow she opened the foil package, ready to slip it over his very thick, very erect cock. She gripped the base, intent on stroking him straight into oblivion, but he grabbed her by the wrist, stopping her.

"I'll come all over your fingers," he warned her, his mouth tight, his eyes narrowed. He was hanging on by a thread, and the power that rippled through her at the realization left her breathless.

She did that to him. She was the one who pushed him so close to the edge he was afraid he'd fall over it with a couple of quick strokes.

Unbelievable.

"Maybe I want you to come all over my fingers," she said, the sound of her husky voice shocking her. She never sounded like that. Never said things like that.

There were a lot of things she'd never experienced before she met Tate.

"Damn, you're sexy as fuck," he said, his hand sliding down over hers as he kissed her. They stroked his cock together, Tate showing her the rhythm that he preferred, squeezing her hand tight around his base. She increased the pace, her thumb gathering liquid from the tip and slicking her grasp. She wanted him to come like this, was desperate to make him lose control, but he wouldn't give in.

Instead he batted her hand away, rolled the condom on himself, and pushed her onto the mattress so he could climb over her. His cock rubbed against her belly, and she scooted up, aligning their bodies better, incredibly eager to feel him push inside her.

"Hurry," she encouraged impatiently, and he did as she asked, his cock poised at her body's entrance just before he thrust his hips up, the head of his cock penetrating her.

He paused, took a deep breath, and then carefully pushed in inch by inch, driving her slowly out of her mind. He was so thick and hard, and she held her breath, clutching at his shoulders as he seemed to take forever before he was fully seated inside her.

She popped her eyes open to find him watching her, sweat dotting his forehead, his lips thin, his jaw tight. She reached up and stroked his cheek, her heart fluttering wildly when he closed his eyes and turned his head so he could kiss her palm. "Are we really doing this?" she asked incredulously.

The sharp laughter that escaped him made her giggle too. "I'm afraid so," he said, his voice deadly serious.

Dipping his head, he brushed her mouth with his, whispering, "You feel so fucking good."

Wren couldn't find the words to express just how good he felt. So she merely said, "You do too."

But those three words seemed good enough.

TATE WAS TRYING to be patient. He wanted to take his time and make sure she was satisfied. But it was proving damn difficult what with the way she squirmed beneath him. Or how her breasts bounced, her pale pink nipples hard, tempting little points he wanted to suck. He was a breast man, he could always admit to that, but damn, he really loved Wren's ass too. In fact, he'd like to flip her over on her knees and fuck her from behind. Would she be down for that? Not tonight but next time? He'd love nothing more but to watch his dick push inside her while she was on her hands and knees, her back arching as she tossed her hair away from her face...

He was getting ahead of himself, thinking of future fucking when he should concentrate on here-and-now fucking. Bracing his hands on the mattress on each side of her head, he circled his hips and thrust deep, holding there for an agonizing moment before he withdrew, then pushed inside again.

She arched beneath him, a tortured sound falling from her swollen lips. He knew it would be good between them but didn't think it would be this good. She wrapped her legs around his hips, her hands gripping his shoulders, and he wound an arm around her waist, pulling her in closer, sending him deeper.

They groaned in unison at the sensation, and he started to fuck her in earnest, their gasping breaths mingling, her feet digging into the small of his back. She felt so damn good, so warm and wet and fucking tight. He pushed and pushed, as if he couldn't get deep enough. Like he couldn't fuck her fast enough, like he couldn't get enough of her. He slipped his fingers between them, searching for and finding her clit. He rubbed quick little circles, her inner walls rippling around his dick, and he knew she was close.

"Come for me, Dove," he urged, and fuck, just like that she did. She cried out, her pussy gripping his cock with enough force to make him see stars, and then he was coming too, groaning her name just before he collapsed on top of her in a shuddering heap.

So much for prolonging the moment.

His bones were liquid as he lay there trying to catch his breath. His heart thundered, roaring in his ears, and he inhaled deeply, taking with him the scent of sex, of sweat, and Wren's citrusy shampoo.

"I'm crushing you," he said when he could finally speak. He started to lift himself off her, but her hands went to his ass, keeping him in place.

"Just a few more minutes," she murmured, her voice muffled by his chest. "I like this."

Ah, Christ. This girl knew just how to burrow in deep and attach herself to him. He liked her—a lot. The sex was phenomenal. She was smart. She seemed to tolerate his bullshit. She made him laugh. She made his dick hard. She kissed him, and he never wanted to stop. And she didn't complain when he came too fast or smashed her into the mattress with his body weight.

He made sure she had an orgasm. They were two for two so far. If she gave him some time to rest, he'd be inclined to see if they could make it three for three.

"I'll be right back," he said a few minutes later before rolling off her and climbing off the bed. He removed the condom and tossed it into the trash can in his bathroom, staring at his reflection in the mirror. The light was off, but he could still see himself thanks to the moonlight filtering through the small window near the ceiling. His hair was a disaster, his eyes were droopy, and his mouth was swollen. He scratched at his chest, glanced down at his—well, what do you know?—semi-erect cock, and was surprised he was still sporting wood.

He didn't look any different, but damn, he felt different. He felt…alive. His skin tingled, and his heart thumped extra hard. That had been, without a doubt, the best sexual experience of his life. He'd kissed her, went down on her while she leaned against the wall in his hallway, and fuck, it had been so damn good. The way she writhed on his lap, stroked his dick, how perfectly their bodies fit, all of it added up to a mind-blowing experience. There hadn't been anything particularly unusual or outrageous about the actual act between them. Truly, it was mostly standard fare, if he was being honest.

But he'd experienced it with *Wren*. That's what pushed it to another level. He liked her. When he touched her, kissed her, it felt like it *meant* something. He just had sex with a girl he cared about. And he wanted more.

He wanted it all.

"Tate," Wren called, interrupting his thoughts. "Come back to bed."

He'd do whatever she wanted, no questions asked.

Smiling, he strode back out into the room, scratching his chest as he approached the bed. Wren had rearranged herself so she was sitting up, propped against a mountain of pillows, the dark blue sheet wrapped tight around her chest and tucked under her arms. Her hair was in complete disarray, and her skin was flushed a rosy pink.

She was…beautiful.

He stopped at the side of the bed, letting his gaze rove over her, his cock magically growing harder by the second just by looking at her.

Wren noticed, her gaze dropping to his dick, her eyes widening before they returned to his. "Already?" she asked, her voice a squeak.

He nodded, reaching down to stroke himself. He wished she was the one stroking him, but he'd settle for his own hand for the moment. "You up for another round?"

She sat up straight and let the sheet fall into a puddle around her waist, exposing her perfect, mouthwatering tits. He was immediately seized with the urge to suck on her nipples. "Okay," she said breathlessly.

Without hesitation he climbed onto the bed and grabbed her, rolling over so she was on top of him, her legs sliding down to wrap around his hips as her hot pussy pressed against his stomach. He rested his hands on her rounded ass, pulling her in so he could feel all that wet, hot warmth on his cock. His eyes nearly crossed at the sensation.

"This time I want to take it slow," he told her, his hands smoothing around to her hips, thumbs sliding down to toy with her pubic hair. "Take my time with you."

"That sounds…perfect," she agreed with an enthusiastic nod, making him chuckle.

He let his hands wander farther, caressing her soft, fragrant skin, enjoying the purrs of pleasure that emanated from her throat. Her hips grew restless, her pussy rubbing against his dick and nearly making him lose his shit. He sat up, drawing one perfect pink nipple between his lips to give it a thorough suck.

"I hope you realize this won't be for just one night," he told her after he released her nipple from his mouth.

She tilted her head down so their gazes met. "What do mean?"

"Us. This." He waved a hand in between them. "It's not a one-time deal."

"All right." She sunk her teeth into her lower lip, blinking at him, looking unsure.

"I want more." He kissed her, sweeping his tongue into her mouth, making her moan when he pulled away. "This is too good to give up on."

Wren kept on blinking, like she couldn't compute what he said. "Wait a minute. Are you serious?"

He nodded, his expression solemn, his heart pounding. He'd never said this sort of stuff to a woman. He wasn't one to make promises he couldn't keep. But Wren…was different. She deserved so much more than he could probably give, but he'd try anyway. He wanted to make her promises. He also wanted to keep them.

He cared about her.

Could see himself falling in love with her if he didn't watch it.

She touched his face, her fingers drifting over his jaw, his chin, coming up to touch his lips. She said nothing, didn't agree that they were too good to give up on, but she didn't protest either. In the end, she merely kissed him, until they were rolling around on the bed wrapped up in each other. They didn't talk. They didn't need to. And when the moment was right and they couldn't stand it any longer, he grabbed another condom and pushed eagerly inside her.

It was good enough. It was fucking great.

He never wanted it to end.

Chapter Sixteen

WREN OPENED TATE's front door to find her two very best friends standing on the front porch, their expressions one of identical concern. "What happened?" she asked, her voice hollow, her legs weak. If they told her something horrible happened to Tate...

She didn't know what she might do.

"Everything's fine," Delilah reassured her, reaching out to pat Wren's arm. "We need to talk though."

Opening the door wider, Wren waved them in. Delilah gave her an apologetic smile. Harper sent her a look that said she believed she was straight-up crazy.

What in the world did that look mean? And what could they want? Wren shut the door and turned the lock into place, counting to three before she faced them with a bright smile. "What's up, ladies?"

"We should be asking you that question," Harper said as she folded her arms in front of her, tapping her foot on the floor. Her sandal slapped loudly on the bare wood, and Delilah winced.

"Harp, stop that," Delilah said.

"No. She needs to explain herself." Harper dropped her arms and glared at Wren. "Start explaining."

"I…" Wren's voice drifted. What in the world could they be mad about? She hadn't told anyone what happened between her and Tate. How wonderful it had been. How it made her feel when he just looked at her, let alone when he touched her. Kissed her. First slipped inside her…

Two nights ago had been the first time they'd had sex, and she still walked around with a dreamy smile on her face, like she was in a stupor. And maybe she was. A Tate-induced stupor, which was a nice place to be. She couldn't wait for him to get off work so they could spend his days off together.

In bed.

Naked.

Harper snapped her fingers, making Wren blink. "Earth to Wren. I can't believe you didn't tell us."

"Well, it just…It happened so fast." She shuffled her feet and glanced down at the floor, her mind a whirlwind of confusion. What was the big deal if she did actually have sex with Tate? They should be thrilled. They'd been pushing her toward him for what felt like forever. It made no sense. Was she not allowed any happiness? That wasn't fair.

Not that life was ever fair, but for once, Wren was starting to think it was actually on her side.

"You think just because Levi comes back into town and sweet-talks you that it's a good idea for you to leave with him? So you can live with him in his fancy mansion?" Harper shook her head and sunk into the dark gray couch, her mouth drawn into a thin line. "That sounds like the worst idea in the world."

"Especially since you're living with Tate," Delilah added as she settled on the couch next to Harper, her gaze full of concern. "I mean, we know you two aren't in a serious relationship or anything, but we were hoping…"

"Wait a minute." Wren settled into the overstuffed chair that sat across from the couch, perching on the edge of the seat. "Did you just say Levi?"

Harper nodded, leaning forward. "Don't play dumb. I spoke to him myself. He was downright giddy, telling me that you were going to go back to San Francisco with him." She hesitated, but then the words burst out like she couldn't stop them. "Are you out of your freaking mind? You can't leave with Levi Hamilton. You're supposed to hate him!"

"I don't hate him." Wren shook her head, amused that her friends would be so concerned with her mental state that they both came over to talk to her. They were always looking out for her best interests, and she appreciated that. Brutal honesty was one of their vows to each other, and right now, Harper was the epitome of brutal honesty.

"You should," Harper practically spit out. "He's a dick."

"Harper," Delilah said, but Harper turned to glare at her.

"What? You know it's true." Harper turned her sharp gaze on Wren. "And you know it's true too. That guy walked all over you. It was all about him throughout your entire relationship. Don't deny it," she said when Wren opened her mouth to protest. "We were young and stupid, and that's your excuse. You will have no excuse if you go back to him. None."

"You don't even know him anymore," Delilah pointed out, her voice much gentler. If they were playing bad cop/good cop, their roles were obvious. "It's been what…ten years since the two of you last talked? A lot of time has passed. The both of you have changed so much."

Wren listened, let them go on about bad choices and leaving the past in the past. She wanted them to get it all out of their system before she told them what was really up. It was almost amusing, how mad they were at her. How they actually thought she'd give everything up to go back to Levi. But she knew if she so much as smiled they'd jump all over her.

So she let them get their concerns out first.

"Are you done?" Wren asked when Harper finally shut up. She'd gone on for at least ten minutes, but it had felt longer.

Harper nodded, her gaze narrowing. "If you're not convinced this is a total mistake yet, I can keep talking. Whatever it takes to keep you here."

Delilah said nothing, just rolled her eyes.

"Why do you want to keep me here?" Wren needed to hear their reasons. Not just for the ego stroke—though that was nice, she couldn't deny it—but because she needed to hear that she was needed. The last few years she'd felt like she'd had no purpose, no meaning. She just worked her little jobs and went about her daily routine, to the point that it had become completely mundane.

No one deserved mundane at the age of twenty-six. That was just so...pitiful.

The only bright spot over the last few months had been her love-hate flirtation with Tate. And now with that turning into something more, something *real*, she was excited. Yes, maybe she was putting everything into a man and the possibility of a relationship, but she had a feeling it would be the right relationship.

"Because we love you," Delilah told her, her gaze downright pleading. "You're our friend, Wren. You're like family. If you choose to leave, then fine, but do so for the right reasons. Not because you think it's the easy way out. Running away from your problems isn't going to solve them."

Ouch. Delilah nailed that one right on the head.

"And running away with Levi won't solve anything," Harper added with a shiver. "He'll only give you more problems."

"You're right," Wren said firmly. "I totally agree with the both of you."

Harper blinked. "You do?"

"Yep." Wren nodded. "I'm sort of pissed that Levi would say that to you, Harper. I never honestly considered his offer."

"You didn't?" Harper squeaked.

Wren shook her head. "Nope." She was mad Levi had told her friends she had though.

"Oh, thank God." Delilah seemed to wilt into the couch, her relief apparent.

"So you're not going to San Francisco to live with Levi?" Harper asked, earning a poke in the ribs from Delilah. She turned on her. "Hey, I was just double-checking."

"No." Wren shook her head, smiling. "I'm so not running away with Levi."

"Good." Harper practically preened. "I knew we could convince her, Dee. Didn't I tell you so?"

"Oh, I'd already made up my mind," Wren added, her smile growing. "Besides, I have Tate now."

Her friends gaped at her, Harper finding her words first. "Um, what do you mean, you have Tate now?"

Wren launched into what happened two nights ago between her and Tate—leaving out most of the supremely naughty parts—but they got the gist. By the time she was wrapping up her story, she was a babbling, blushing mess, and both Delilah and Harper were watching her with lovesick expressions on their faces.

"That is the sweetest thing ever," Delilah said, clasping her hands together. She looked ready to swoon. "He actually told you that he wasn't going to give up on you?"

Wren nodded, still amazed he would say such a thing. "I know we haven't known each other that long, but…"

"When you know, you know," Harper said. "And it sounds like Tate…knows."

"Don't jump to conclusions. It's way too early in our relationship." Wren frowned. "I don't even know if I can call it a relationship."

"You're living in his house," Delilah pointed out. "And you're having sex. Sounds like a relationship to me."

Oh God. Delilah was right. They were in a relationship.

"It's nothing serious," Wren said, wincing the moment the words left her.

"Are you serious right now?" Harper asked incredulously.

Wren shrugged, feeling silly. Okay, maybe she was still feeling insecure. Everything between her and Tate was still so new. And she was still so unsure about—everything. She still had no home and nothing really to her name. Her entire life was up in the air, and she had no idea where it was all going to land, but she felt somehow secure, knowing that she had Tate in her life. Standing by her side. Keeping her steady, keeping her safe.

Making her feel cared for.

"We love that you and Tate are giving this a go. I mean, compared to Levi…" Harper's voice drifted, and she shot a guilty look in Delilah's direction.

"What?" Wren asked, staring at her friends. Hard. Like that could make them talk. "Spit out what you want to say."

"Levi is still just a silly little boy looking for someone to stroke his ego," Harper explained, rolling her eyes. "Yeah, yeah, he's created some app that made him a millionaire or whatever, but he still acts like a kid. He's just an adolescent boy inside a man's body who gets his rocks off by surrounding himself with people who constantly feed his ego."

"Exactly." Delilah nodded in agreement. "But Tate? He may act cocky sometimes. And he knows he's gorgeous. But he's a man who takes care of his own. He's a freaking hero every single day that he goes to work. And it sounds like he's a total goner for you. Why would you want to be with anyone else when you could be with Tate?"

Wren couldn't help but totally agree.

THE STATION PHONE rang, startling Tate out of his stupor. Three days into his four-day shift and it had been nonstop. The tourists were out in droves, and they were reckless as hell. He'd been on countless medical aid calls, wellness checks, and the occasional fire, all of them small and easy to put out, thank God. But he was exhausted. They all were.

Hence they were all indulging in a little siesta time after lunch. They'd gone on a middle-of-the-night call and didn't stumble back into the station until around four in the morning. He'd been dozing in his bed, his thoughts full of a naked Wren, when the annoying shrill of the phone ringing busted through his pleasant dreams.

He ran out into the hall and answered the phone, hoping everyone else was at least still napping.

"It was arson," Josh said as greeting. "It's been confirmed."

Tate frowned, his exhausted brain not fully computing. "What was arson?"

"The house fire at Wren Gallagher's residence. I was wrong. It wasn't caused accidentally." It sounded like it took a lot for ol' grumpy Bailey to just admit that he was wrong. Lucky for him, Tate wasn't in the mood to rub his face in it. "The same accelerant used to cause the other fires was also used at her residence."

Dread pooled in the pit of Tate's stomach, and he swallowed hard. "So what do you think? Was this something personal or what?"

"I don't know what to think or if Wren was targeted," Josh started, but Tate interrupted him.

"Of course she was targeted. Why else would her house be the only residential structure that was included in our arsonist's so-called 'projects'?" Tate ran a hand through his hair and looked around the empty hallway, feeling helpless. Damn it, he wanted to rush home to Wren right now and hold her in his arms. Protect her from whoever was after her. What if the asshole was *still* after her? "Do you think she's being followed?"

"I don't know. I doubt it, but I already talked to Lane Gallagher, and he's on it." Josh's voice was grim. "He's going to put a tag on her, which will probably be himself. See if someone could potentially be following her."

"Christ." Tate closed his eyes for a brief moment and pressed his forehead against the wall. He couldn't imagine anyone wanting to harm Wren. She was a good girl. Solid and smart and kind to everyone—except for him, but that was when she believed he was a player. "This is all sorts of fucked up."

"Tell me about it," Josh muttered. "There have been no more new leads and no more new fires since Wren's. I don't know if he got scared because of the totality of the house fire or if he's just…given up."

"Keep dreaming. He hasn't given up. I think he's far from finished," Tate said, pushing away from the wall and accidentally getting wound up in the telephone cord. Damn phone was older than he was, but the state of California refused to replace it. Besides, even he could grudgingly admit it still worked just fine. "More like he's quietly biding his time while planning his next move."

And if the arsonist's next move included Wren…

Tate frowned. If her life was in danger, if something happened to her, he'd never forgive himself. Ever.

"If that's the case, she's in safe hands, what with her family and who they are," Josh said. "Maybe she should move back in with her parents. At least her dad is there all the time."

Tate remained quiet. Her father had been the idol of pretty much every firefighter in the ranger unit, especially about fifteen, twenty years ago. Until he became a no-good, cheating bastard who drank too much and ignored his wife and kids. He retired early, went out on disability, and spent his days sulking, drinking, or fishing.

"She's at my place," Tate finally said. "She's safe there." He wanted her nowhere else. Hell, he wanted to leave work early so he could go see her. Make sure she was okay.

"But you're at the station most of the time. Lane can't follow her around twenty-four/seven," Josh pointed out.

"And her dad can't keep tabs on her every hour of the day either. She's not stupid. She'll keep herself safe. Plus she'd notice anything suspicious, especially once we tell her what's going on."

Josh breathed deep. "See, that's the thing. Her brothers don't want us telling her what's going on."

"Say what?" Tate lowered his voice, hoping he hadn't woken anyone. "Are you fucking kidding me?"

"I'm not. Lane and West both asked that I specifically not tell her the cause of the fire was arson," Josh said.

"That's ridiculous. I already told her I thought it was arson. She *needs* to know. Maybe she saw something, or maybe she *will* see something." Hell. Her brothers were just trying to protect her, but she deserved to know. She wasn't a little girl they needed to take care of anymore. Her life could potentially be in danger, and her big brothers wanted to keep her in the dark? That was the stupidest thing he'd ever heard. "I'm going to tell her."

"Don't you fucking dare," Josh said, sounding worried. He was probably afraid of a Gallagher tag-team ass kicking. Tate really couldn't blame him, but still. This was some straight-up bullshit. "Just…not yet. Give them a few days to cool down. Then you can talk some sense into their heads and get them to see your reasoning. I'm on your side with this one," he grudgingly admitted. "She deserves to know what's going on. She could possibly help us find the arsonist."

"Right." Tate sighed, the sound ragged. He didn't want to agree to this. It went against everything he believed in. "Fine. I'll keep my lips shut. But I'm off in a little over twenty-four hours. If no one has told her yet, I will. Swear to God. I'm not going to keep her in the dark about this. It's too dangerous to keep from her."

"I get it. I do, and I agree. Go talk to West and Lane. Convince them that they need to tell her what's up. She'll figure out something is weird if she spots Lane following her all the time anyway. He's just some small-time cop. How stealthy can he be?"

Tate would've laughed any other time over Josh insulting Lane. The arson investigator didn't like the Gallagher brothers, and the feeling was mutual. Even Holden thought Josh was an asshole, and he was rarely around the guy. But those Gallaghers held strong together. They took care of their own—sometimes to the point of overdoing it.

ONCE TATE ENDED the call with Josh, he knew his nap time was over. He went outside to call Wren on his cell, needing to hear her voice and reassure himself that she was okay.

"Hey, you," she answered, sounding shy. It was obvious she still wasn't sure how to treat him after they'd had sex. Her uncertainty was cute.

"What's up, Dove?" She sighed irritably at his nickname, and he smiled. "You should be glad Woodpecker didn't stick."

"I wish none of them had stuck," she said, but he didn't believe her. Deep down inside, he knew she was a fan of Dove. Of all of the bird nicknames, even Woodpecker. "How are you?"

"I'm good." He paused. "How are you? What's new?"

She told him about hanging out with Delilah and Harper—and how she told her friends about what happened between them. "But I didn't give them all the dirty details," she rushed to add. "Just that we…you know."

"Banged all night long?" he supplied for her.

"Right." She laughed. "You make it sound so seedy."

"Okay. We made love till morning light?"

More laughter, and the sound made his chest tighten. Damn, this girl. She had a way of changing his mood for the better no matter what. "That's cheesy."

"I give up. You describe it."

"You want me to...what?"

"If we didn't bang, and we didn't make love, then what was it?" Now he was just egging her on, trying to make her squirm.

He had a feeling it was working too.

"We...had sex," she said, her voice small.

"Oh, come on, Wren. I know you can get more creative than that."

"Um, we messed around?"

"Try again."

"You went down on me?"

Okay. That worked. "Don't forget I finger-fucked you too."

"Tate." She said his name like she wanted him to keep his voice down.

"Wren."

"You're incorrigible."

"That's my most endearing trait."

A wistful sigh escaped her, the sound going straight to his dick. "Maybe."

"We also fucked," he reminded her. "That night. We fucked a lot."

"That word is so crude."

"What word? *Fucking*? I like it."

"I can tell," she retorted.

"Say it for me, Dove."

"What?" she practically shrieked. Now it was his turn to chuckle.

"Say the word. I want to hear it come from your delectable lips."

"You think my lips are delectable?"

"I think every single thing about you is delectable." That was the 100 percent truth.

"Aw, you're too sweet." She hesitated. "And you're right. We definitely—fucked a lot that night."

"Ah, there you go." If they kept this up, he would end up with a boner tenting the front of his uniform pants. And that wouldn't be cool considering he was in a station full of mostly guys. "It sounds hot coming from you, baby."

"I like it when you call me baby," she admitted in a whisper.

"Well, I'll call you baby while I fuck you all night long, okay? Hold on to that thought."

"Are we having phone sex, Tate?"

"Not quite." He chuckled, knew that she was kidding with him. "But if you want to, I'm down."

"You're down for anything."

"You're damn right." He heard a door slam and turned to see some of the firefighters emerge outside, all of them blinking against the bright sunlight. "Gotta go. The troops are rising from their siesta."

"Ah, nap time. I hope you got some sleep."

Guilt crept over him when he remembered what woke him up from his nap—and how he couldn't tell her. But he would. Soon he planned on telling her everything. "A little bit. Hopefully we'll have an uneventful night, and I can actually have uninterrupted sleep."

"Is that what you're looking forward to when you come home? An uneventful night?" she teased.

"With you naked in my bed, baby? It's going to be the most eventful night of fucking you've ever experienced," he said confidently.

"You promise?"

"I fucking guarantee it."

Chapter Seventeen

WREN DROVE OVER to the BFD after calling in her order, feeling guilty for not making a healthy dinner. She'd copped out by buying a cheeseburger and fry basket to go instead. But screw it. She went jogging with Delilah earlier this morning—big mistake. Delilah ran her into the ground. The girl was beyond fit and had endless stamina. After their exhausting run, when Wren had been gasping and ready to collapse onto the ground, she'd told Delilah her brother must be a lucky man to have her in his life.

Delilah only smiled mysteriously in answer—which was enough of an answer for Wren. She didn't like to think of her friend and her brother getting freaky together, and she had to multiply that by two considering Harper and West were also getting freaky with each other. It sucked because her friends' new boyfriends, a.k.a. her brothers, took all the sex talk out of their friendship equation.

Which was why both of her friends were so eager to hear details about her and Tate. Since Wren refused to talk about their sex lives—ew, she didn't want to hear sexual escapades involving West or Lane—they wanted to hear all about her and Tate.

They hounded her with questions every chance they got. And considering they'd known about the sex thing for only the last, hmm…forty-eight hours or so? It was amazing just how much they'd bombarded her with endless digs and comments, curious questions, and sexual innuendo.

But she soaked it all up, secretly enjoying it. When was the last time she had juicy tidbits to share? Oh, she didn't tell them *everything*. No way could she reveal Tate's penis size—large. Or that particular trick he did with his tongue on her…

Hmm. Her skin grew hot just thinking about that tongue trick.

As she pulled into the Bigfoot Diner parking lot, she glanced in her rearview mirror just in time to see a dark sedan enter the lot behind her. She frowned, watching it pull into a spot at the far end of the lot, then turned her engine off. She swore that same car had been following her earlier, when she drove back to Tate's from the dance studio. If it wasn't that exact car, it was an eerily similar one.

Weird.

She exited her car and went into the restaurant, waving a greeting at Harper's grandma, who was behind the counter cutting a piece of peach pie for one of the longtime residents of Wildwood. He was an old grumpy dude who came into the BFD practically every day, and Harper insisted he was hot for her grandma.

Most of the older single men in Wildwood were hot for Harper's grandma, so this didn't surprise Wren at all.

She paid for her meal at the hostess stand, grabbed the to-go sack, and bounded out of the diner, practically running to her car. She was eager to get home so she could eat. Her stomach growled at the aroma coming from the paper bag, and she recalled that she'd skipped lunch after feeling guilty for eating two chocolate doughnuts before her run with Delilah.

Yeah. She needed to reevaluate her eating habits— they sucked, and she wasn't getting any younger. She had a high metabolism now, but that could all go to hell by the time she was thirty. Maybe Tate could help her with that. He was in excellent shape, with abs that made her feel like a lesser human being. And while normally that would give her a major hang-up, right now she was reveling in it because, damn it, those were *her* abs to explore and touch with her hands and lips and tongue.

Smiling, she drove back to Tate's house with the radio cranked up, singing as loud as she could to the latest summer hit. There was always one song people could count on to remind them of a particular summer, and this year was no exception. Every time she heard the song, she thought of Tate. Not of her house burning down or her friends giving her grief or her worry over her future and how tempted she'd been by that crazy offer from Levi…

Funny, how she never heard from him again after that long coffee date, which had happened days ago. He was probably back in San Francisco by now. Good riddance. This was the summer of Tate, not Levi.

Just thinking about Tate made her stomach flutter. His naughty smile every time he called her by a different bird nickname. The glow in his eyes when he'd stared at her that night in his hallway, just before he kissed her for the first time. Oh, and how he kissed, so thoroughly obliterating her brain cells until she was nothing but a boneless heap slumped against a wall. He was a master orgasm provider too. She'd come three times that night— or had it been four? Yeah, *four* times, good grief. A girl would be stupid to let go of a man who had a record like that. Though he had other redeeming qualities too…

Plenty of them. Too many to mention. She just flat out liked the man. Liked the way he made her feel, and that was important. Levi had always made her feel like she was second best. The other men she'd dated in the past had done much the same, putting their jobs and themselves ahead of her every single time.

Not Tate. He seemed focused on only her. He had a job that he was passionate about, but he was passionate about her too. And that was heady stuff.

She pulled into Tate's driveway and cut the engine, climbing out of the car with the paper bag from the BFD clutched tightly in her fingers. It was already starting to get dark. Tate would come home tomorrow. She'd been on the phone with him earlier, and they ended up talking for over an hour, planning what they'd do once he was off for three days—it sounded like all he wanted was her. In bed. Naked.

She was fine with that.

Smiling to herself, she hit the keyless remote to lock her car and headed for the front door, a little thrill zipping down her spine as her fingers slid over the key to Tate's house. She was being silly, thinking it meant something that they lived together, when really he was just being a friend at the time he offered, but still. They were *living* together. And even though the plan was that she would be there for only a short while, they were getting along—rather well was probably an understatement.

She understood the life of being with a firefighter. She'd grown up the daughter of one; she knew what their hectic schedules were like. If they could make this work and turn it into something real…

The sound of a car approaching made her pause in the middle of the walkway, and she turned toward the street, waiting for the car to pass, curious to check it out. Tate lived in a cul-de-sac, and not many cars drove down the short road beyond the few neighbors he had. When she saw that it was the same dark sedan from earlier at the BFD, everything inside her went cold.

And then everything went into motion.

Wren darted for the front door, practically tripping over her feet as she flew up the porch's short steps. Her hands shaking, she tried to stick the key into the front door and missed, cursing under her breath as she glanced over her shoulder. Damn it, she just wanted to get inside and call 911. Or maybe she should call Lane directly? He'd probably get there faster. Was he on duty tonight? God, she had no idea, though she used to keep track of his schedule. Why, she wasn't sure.

Stop thinking about stupid shit, and get inside!

She leaned against the door and slipped the key into the dead bolt and turned it, feeling it give a little under her weight. She shoved the door open and slipped inside, slamming the door and turning the lock with satisfying brute force. Dropping the bag of food on the coffee table, she grabbed her phone out of her purse and dialed Lane's number. Going to the window, she peeked through the edge of the curtain to watch as the sedan sat idling in front of Tate's house. The engine shut off, as did the lights at the precise moment Lane answered her call.

"Wren, what's going on?"

His answer made her rear back a little. "How do you know something's going on?"

Lane cleared his throat, sounding irritated. "Uh, why are you calling me? Is everything okay?"

"Someone's following me," she whispered, her heart threatening to burst out of her chest when she saw the driver's side door of the sedan open and the shadow of a very tall man climb out of the car. The rapidly descending darkness made it hard for her to make out his features. "Oh my God, he's at my house! He got out of his car. I think…shit, I don't know what to think."

"Hold on. I'll be there in a minute," Lane said grimly.

"A minute? Where exactly are you?" Her throat went dry, and she let the curtain fall back into place, not wanting to see this guy come toward her house.

Then again, she might need to notice details for whatever police report she was going to have to give.

"At the corner of Tate's street. Hold on." She heard the squeal of tires on pavement, Lane muttering something under his breath that sounded like a string of curse words. Why in the world was he so close? It made no sense.

She heard the squeal of tires again, both over the phone and right outside. Reaching out, she pulled the curtain back to see another plain sedan pull up behind the first one. Lane leapt out of the driver's side and ran toward Tate's front yard. He tackled the guy as he approached the porch, taking him down onto the ground with a muffled grunt.

That she managed to hear, because somehow Lane still had the phone in his hand.

Unlocking and throwing open the door, she flicked on the light and went onto the front porch, watching in disbelief as Lane struggled with the stranger. The man had his arms bent in front of his face as if to protect himself, and he wore a pair of crisp khaki shorts and a white polo shirt.

Realization dawned, and Wren placed trembling fingers over her mouth. She knew exactly who that was.

"Lane! Get off him! It's Levi!"

Lane whipped his head toward her, his expression fierce. "Get back inside," he practically growled as he straddled Levi like he was about to choke him out.

"No!" She ran across the porch and down the steps, tugging at Lane's shoulder. He wasn't even in uniform. So what the hell was he doing patrolling around here?

"Lane, come on. It's my old high school boyfriend. Stop trying to beat him up."

Her oldest brother paused, squinting down at Levi, who still covered his face with his arms. "Look at me," he demanded, shaking Levi's shoulders.

Levi slowly dropped his arms, the pure terror on his face obvious. "I wasn't going to hurt her. I just wanted to talk," he said feebly.

"Jesus," Lane muttered, grabbing hold of Levi's shirt and giving him a shove before he stood. He turned to look at Wren. "He's been following you for hours."

She gaped at Lane. "How do you know?"

"Because *I've* been following you for hours." He glared at Levi as he drew himself to his feet, brushing off the front of his pristine shirt and shorts. "What the hell are you doing back in town anyway?"

"I wanted to talk to you," Levi said to her, ignoring Lane. "But you haven't answered my calls."

Wren glanced down at her notification-less phone. "You haven't called me."

"I have too."

"You should've texted me."

"I've done that as well."

She held her phone out to him. "Hate to tell you this then, but maybe you've been texting and calling the wrong number?"

Lane approached them, pushing his hair out of his face. "Are you sure you're all right with this joker being here?" He jerked his thumb in Levi's direction.

"Hold on," she told Levi before dragging Lane a few feet away, out into the yard. "Explain exactly why you've been following me."

"It's a long story," he said with a sigh.

"Oh, trust me. I have all night." She crossed her arms in front of her chest, forgetting all about her hunger and the delicious cheeseburger and fries she had waiting for her inside. "Fess up." She reached out and poked him in the chest with her index finger, making him back up a step. "Now."

Shaking his head, Lane exhaled loudly. "It's nothing, Wren, I swear. I just…wanted to make sure you were safe."

"Why? Am I in danger?" A sense of foreboding sent a shiver down her spine.

"Listen, Wren. I have to go." Levi was suddenly there, his hand on her arm as he stepped in between her and Lane. She could feel her big brother glaring at him, but Levi acted completely unfazed. Probably didn't even notice Lane's potent anger. So typical. "But I want to talk to you first."

"We were already talking, asshole," Lane muttered, and Wren glared at him.

"Stop, Lane. Give us a minute," she told her brother before she walked back toward the house with Levi. "What's going on?" she asked him.

"I'm such an idiot. I followed you around this afternoon, trying to work up the nerve to talk to you, but I never could." He smoothed his hand over his jaw, wincing when he touched a particular spot.

"And when I finally did work up the nerve, your brother jumps out of his car like some sort of renegade cop and tackles me to the ground," Levi muttered, brushing off the front of his very clean polo shirt one more time.

If he kept that up, she'd have to ask him to stop, because it was completely irritating and made him seem like a total sissy.

"Did he hurt you?" she asked.

Levi shook his head reluctantly. "I'm fine. Just startled more than anything."

She couldn't make herself say *sorry*. That was for Lane to do, though she knew he wouldn't. "What did you want to talk about?"

"My offer. Did you consider it?" he asked hopefully.

"I did." She hesitated, and the light dimmed from his eyes, like she just snuffed out a candle. "I...I can't do it, Levi. We had our teenage moment years ago, and it was great, but we can never return to that sort of relationship. I'd like us to remain friends though."

Sighing, he slipped his hands into his pockets and offered her a sad smile. "I understand. I expected too much. Probably got caught up in memories more than anything else."

"Probably," she agreed, not letting his comment sting. He was being honest, as was she. And she had Tate. She didn't need Levi.

"I'm sorry if I scared you. That was never my intent." He reached out for her, then dropped his arms, seemingly embarrassed. She went to him instead and hugged him close.

"I'm thrilled that you've found so much success, Levi. I'm sure someday soon you'll find a special woman to share it with," she murmured close to his ear.

"Thanks, Wren." He squeezed her before he let her go and stepped away. "Take care, okay?"

"You too. Are you headed back to San Francisco now?"

"Yeah, wanted to leave tonight. Need to get back to work in the morning." The answer and his sheepish smile revealed what she'd suspected. Her ex was a complete workaholic. He would probably make a girl extremely happy someday, but right now, he was devoted to his job. "Let's keep in touch?"

"Let's make sure you have the right phone number for me first," she suggested.

They discovered the number he entered for her was off by one digit, and they got a good laugh out of it before he left town for good. She watched his car disappear down the street and then turned her attention to Lane. He was leaning against his car, tapping away on his phone.

"You're not off the hook," she told him.

He glanced up from his phone with a grimace. "I did nothing wrong, Wren. More like I was in the right place at the right time."

"Whatever. I'm eating my dinner, and you're going to explain to me exactly what's going on," she told him as she started for the front door.

"I gotta get home," he protested, but she silently glared at him, earning a muttered—and reluctant—*all right* as he followed her to the front door.

She was determined to get to the bottom of Lane's odd behavior before the night was over.

Chapter Eighteen

WREN GAPED AT her brother, trying her best to come up with something to say but failing miserably. What he was telling her was unbelievable.

Oh, and maddening—completely and totally infuriating, really.

She was sitting at Tate's tiny kitchen table with her oldest brother, trying to eat her dinner while listening to Lane explain the craziest story she'd ever heard. Why would someone be after her? What had she ever done to anyone? Absolutely nothing.

That's why what Lane said made no sense.

"Tate and Josh wanted to tell you right away," Lane said after he informed her that the reason her house burned down was because of the Wildwood arsonist—and they believed she might've been specifically targeted. "But West and I thought it best if we kept you out of it for a little while. See if we could finally nab the arsonist first before you had to get—involved."

Swallowing hard, she finally found her voice. "So you believed it was…what? In my best interests I was kept in the dark about some nut job who burned down my house and, oh, I don't know, might still be after me? That sounded like a good idea to you and West, the overlords of my life? Really?"

Lane winced. "When you put it like that…"

"You're an asshole," she said, interrupting him. She slapped the edge of the table, hurting her fingers in the process. *Great.* "And so is West. Did you two really think I wouldn't be able to handle it? Like I'm some delicate flower who'd freak out if she knew a big, bad, scary man burned her house down on purpose?"

"We only just confirmed that," he rushed to add.

"Whatever." She wrapped up her half-eaten cheeseburger and stuffed it back into the bag. She'd lost her appetite over this conversation. She was too mad to eat. Her brothers were so damn controlling. They always had been, and it made her furious.

And deep down, it hurt. Did they really believe she couldn't take care of herself? Had she made such bad choices throughout her life that they had no faith in her? Yeah, she'd messed up a time or two when she was a teen, but nothing major. It had been a stage. She usually played it safe—to the point it might have made her life a little boring sometimes. But she'd always believed boring was better than scary.

This summer, though, had been the most exciting one she'd had in a long time. Yeah, the fire was a dark moment, but it had brought her something good. It forced her to get closer to Tate. She didn't regret that for a moment.

"We only wanted to protect you." Lane reached out and touched her arm, but she pulled away from his grasp. He scowled at her. "We thought we were doing what was best."

"For you or for me?" she snipped.

"You. Always you. The thought of some creep burning down your house on purpose." Lane's mouth set in a firm line. "Hell, Wren, it's freaking spooky." He shook his head, his expression menacing. "I should've never let Levi go. He could've been the one who burned your house down."

Lane was totally reaching. "Give me a break. He was only home for a few days. Are you saying he traveled back and forth between here and San Francisco throughout the summer just to burn Wildwood down? Why would he even do that?"

"I don't know. He's pissed at the town in general?" Lane shrugged. "He never did like this place much."

"Neither did West. Maybe he's the arsonist."

"Now you're just being ridiculous," Lane muttered.

"No, *you're* being ridiculous, what with your overbearing protectiveness and sense of what's right and wrong." She paused, hoping he understood just how hurt and upset she was over this. "You should've never kept it from me, Lane. You and West don't get to make decisions that affect my life in such a big way, you know. I'm my own person. I can take care of myself."

"We can take care of you too."

"And I appreciate that. I do. But sometimes you two are so overbearing. I don't know how Tate will put up with you two jerks considering we're now…" She paused, frowning. Considering they were now…what? In a relationship? That sounded too serious. Fucking around? That sounded too casual, and no way could she use those particular words with Lane. He'd flip.

"Considering you're what with Tate?" Lane's eyes narrowed as he watched her.

She sighed and waved a dismissive hand, trying not to make too big a deal out of this. "We're sort of—seeing each other?" There. That worked.

"Uh-huh." Lane nodded, his expression still grim. "I thought that might be the case, especially with the way Tate talked to me yesterday."

Curiosity had her frowning. "What exactly did you two talk about?"

His expression immediately turned guilty. "The house fire and how it was set by the arsonist."

Her head started to spin. Tate knew about it too? Wait, her brother had mentioned he knew. So why didn't Tate tell her? Was he supposedly trying to protect her as well? God, he was just like them. "So Tate knew that the fire was started by the arsonist too?"

"Um, well…yeah." Lane shrugged, looking caught, just like the rat he was. More like there were three rats involved in this crazy secret-keeping scheme. Her two older brothers and much to her disappointment…

Tate.

"He wanted to tell you," Lane added. "But we wouldn't let him."

Wren said nothing. Tate was a grown-ass man, yet he couldn't work up the nerve to go against her brothers' wishes and tell her the truth? Whose side was he on anyway?

Clearly, her brothers'.

"You should go." Wren stood and gathered up the garbage from her dinner, tossing it into the trash. She went to the kitchen sink and washed her hands, keeping her back to Lane. She didn't want to look at him anymore.

She wanted him gone.

"Come on, Wren. You can't be too upset. We were just watching out for you," Lane said, his tone pleading. He didn't like it when she was mad at him. Much like she didn't like it when he was mad at her. They'd always had a close relationship, even when they were kids and she followed him everywhere, driving him crazy. She always figured he secretly liked her obvious adulation for her big brother.

But right now, she wanted to kick her big brother's ass. It didn't matter that he could probably snap her in two. Lane was so big and broad and downright menacing when he wanted to be. She was so pissed she was tempted to give it a go, knowing he would never stop her.

Punching him would probably end with her hurting her hands. If she tried to kick him, she'd probably miss or, worse, injure herself. The man was a powerhouse.

She, on the other hand, ate doughnuts for breakfast and cheeseburgers for dinner.

"I want you to leave." She turned away from the sink and folded her arms in front of her chest, staring her brother down. "I want to be alone."

"Aw, come on, Wren," he started as he stood, but she shook her head.

"No. Don't try to wear me down or tell me I'm being silly. I'm mad, Lane. You and West—and Tate—must really think I'm stupid, that I can't handle this." It hurt to include Tate in that short list. She was furious with her brothers—West should consider himself lucky he wasn't here—but she was devastated by Tate's decision to keep this from her. Yes, he had a job to do, and some things would always need to be kept quiet.

But this involved her. She thought she meant enough to Tate that he would treat her with respect and let her know when—*hello*—her life was in danger.

She guessed she was wrong. And that's what hurt the most.

TATE UNLOCKED THE front door and walked inside his house, breathing deep the scent of freshly brewed coffee. Knowing that Wren was somewhere in the house made his steps lighter and his heart pound. He couldn't wait to see her. Wrap her up in his arms and kiss her. Push her into bed and have his way with her.

Yeah, that was the plan for the day. Naked bedtime. He hoped she was still down with that.

He set his bag down by the door and headed for the kitchen, hoping she was in there. Maybe she was making him breakfast. Maybe she was sitting at the table sipping a cup of coffee, her hair tousled and her eyes sleepy, wearing one of his T-shirts. That sounded nice. That sounded better than nice.

But when he entered the kitchen, she wasn't there. Only the coffeemaker greeted him, percolating noisily as it finished brewing the coffee.

Pushing aside the disappointment that crashed through him, Tate left the kitchen and started down the hall toward his bedroom. Maybe she was in his shower. Now, that was a beyond-pleasant thought. A naked, soapy Wren under a stream of steaming-hot water was a fantasy he hadn't had yet. He could help her get clean, assist her with those hard-to-reach places. Only if she would do the same for him…

She wasn't in the shower. She wasn't in his bedroom either. Nope, she was back in the guest room, fully dressed in shorts and a T-shirt, her hair swept up into a tight ponytail, the bed neatly made.

Her gym bag she used to keep at Delilah's dance studio sat on top of the bed. She set a stack of folded clothes inside, turning on a gasp when he rapped on the doorframe. "Oh." She rested her hand against her chest. "You scared me."

"You knew I was coming home." He leaned against the doorjamb. "I texted you."

"Right." She dropped her hand and nodded, her expression noncommittal. It was devoid of any emotion, even her eyes, which was…weird. Wren was the most expressive woman he knew.

When she didn't say anything else, icy-cold unease trickled down his spine. "What's going on, Dove?"

She lifted her chin, a hint of defiance making an appearance. Christ, she was beautiful, even without a lick of makeup on. He liked her best in her natural state, especially in her naked natural state, but clearly something was wrong. He had a feeling he wouldn't be seeing her in his favorite naked state today.

"Do you have something you want to tell me?" she asked, her voice crisp.

"Uh…" He searched his mind, which had been fully occupied with the various sexual positions he wanted to try out with Wren only a few seconds ago.

"Maybe about the fire?" she suggested helpfully.

Dread filled him. He didn't like the overly pleasant tone of voice. Or the way she watched him, like she wanted to jump on him and scratch his eyes out with her fingernails. Fuck. Did she find out about the circumstances behind her house fire?

"I discovered that Lane was following me," she said, giving him a pointed look. "And that the reason for his following me has to do with the arsonist being the one who burned my house down. He mentioned that he and West thought it was a good idea to keep it from me—and that you agreed."

"I never fucking said that," he said vehemently, making her back up a step. Damn it, he didn't mean to sound so angry. "I didn't agree with their decision to keep it from you."

"Yet you did anyway. Even when you told me in the first place that the fire was arson."

Right. He'd never denied it. So why was she angry? "I fully planned on telling you today. Right now." Well. He would've kissed her first. Touched her. Dragged her into bed and given her a few orgasms before finally informing her of what was up. "I told Josh and I told your brothers it was messed up that they were keeping this from you."

"But you kept it from me too, Tate." He started to protest, but she cut him off. "I know you told me you thought it was arson right after it happened, but when they asked you to keep quiet about the recent details, you went along with them. And kept it secret from me."

"I said I'd agree with their decision until I was off. The moment I came home, I planned on telling you everything."

"You should've told me from the very first moment they told you. That's what *couples* do. They don't keep secrets from each other." She turned so her back was to him and started shoving the rest of the piles of clothes into her bag. "I should come before them."

"You do." He went to her, touching her shoulders, but they stiffened beneath his hands, and he let them drop. "I knew it was a bad idea, keeping this from you."

"So why didn't you tell me?" She whirled around to face him, standing so close he could smell her. He wanted to bury his face in her neck and never let her go. "You should've fought harder to make your point. I deserved to know."

"They were your brothers. I thought they knew best," he said, knowing his reasoning sounded weak. Shit, maybe it was weak. She was putting doubt in his head, making him feel like shit, and he probably deserved it. But damn it, he never wanted to hurt her. He wanted to protect her.

Always.

"I'm a grown woman who can take care of herself. Clearly, the men in my life believe otherwise." She turned toward the bed again and zipped her bag closed before grabbing the handle and slinging it over her shoulder. "I'm leaving."

"Where are you going?"

"To Delilah's. She's never there anyway, considering she's always with Lane." Tate stood directly in front of her, and she glared up at him. "Get out of my way."

"No." He shook his head. "Let me explain first."

"There's nothing to explain. You thought I couldn't take care of myself. You're probably right. So maybe I need to spend some time on my own until I can figure all of this out."

"Figure all of what out?" He frowned, wishing he could keep her. He just wanted Wren. Nothing else mattered if he couldn't have her in his life.

"This. My life. It's kinda pitiful, don't you think?" She flashed him a fake smile, then shoved past him, startling him so bad that it took him a second before he chased after her.

"Wren, don't go." He grabbed hold of her arm, and she turned to face him, the anger and hurt he saw blazing in her eyes nearly crushing him. "Let me explain."

"Explain what? That you think I can't handle the truth? That I'm just a pretty little girl who needs to be taken care of? I'm not scared of the arsonist supposedly targeting me. That's the craziest thing I've ever heard. What bothers me the most is that you didn't side with me. You sided with my brothers. I never come first in my family, and I guess I don't come first with you either."

Jesus, how did this get so twisted up? He thought she might be mad that they kept this from her but not this mad. "You're not being fair."

"Neither were you. I deserved to know. You should've gone against my brothers' wishes and told me. If you really…cared"—she stumbled over the last word—"you would've."

He ran his fingers down her arm, but she jerked away from him. How could he calm her down and make her see his side if she was so angry? "I'm sorry," he said, taking a step closer to her. "I fucked up. I never meant to hurt you, I promise. I just…I wanted to make sure you were safe. So did your brothers. We just wanted to protect you."

"I don't need this kind of protection." She sniffed, and he swore he saw tears filling her eyes, but she blinked them away. "Good-bye, Tate."

Before he could say another word, she turned and walked away from him, headed straight for the door. Headed straight out of his life.

And he didn't know how to stop her.

Chapter Nineteen

"YOUR MISERY IS making me crazy," Delilah muttered as she kicked at Wren's foot. "Get off your ass, and let's go for a run."

"Hell no," Wren muttered, shaking her head. She was sulking on the couch in Delilah's living room, eating straight out of an ice cream carton and watching *Judge Judy*. It made her feel better that her life wasn't as bad as some of the people who were on this trashy show, airing their dirty laundry for all the world to see.

"Then stop stuffing your face with ice cream, and talk to me." Delilah sat next to her and swiped the spoon right out of Wren's hand.

"Hey," she protested. Delilah then plucked the carton of ice cream out of Wren's other hand and set both on the side table next to her. "Give that back."

"No." Delilah shook her head, her ponytail swinging. She looked like her usual perfect self, dressed in a pair of black booty shorts and a pink sports-bra-top thing. She'd just come back from the dance studio after giving classes for the last two hours, and Wren wanted to punch Dee in her perfectly flat stomach. Ugh, her friend's perfect body was just too much. "You need to stop sulking and start living. Look for a new place. Get your hair cut. Buy some clothes, plan a shopping day at IKEA for your future new place. Go out with Harper and me. Do something to get yourself out of your miserable head."

A week had passed since she walked out of Tate's house. Seven long, miserable days, and she wasn't feeling any better about her rash decision. No, she felt worse. Maybe she shouldn't have walked out on him after all. She probably should've listened to his explanation. She knew how overbearing her brothers could be. But she'd been so offended, so upset they'd think she couldn't handle such bad news, she'd reacted instead of being proactive.

A habit she used to have when she was younger, thanks to her bossy older brothers. Their behavior reminded her so much of the past that she fell back into bad habits. Not a smart move. Had she lost Tate for good? He tried to call and text her the day she left, and the next day too. But then he went back to work—and his engine got called out on a big fire in Northern California. He was still gone, and she had no idea when he was coming back.

Had no idea if he would ever contact her again either.

And that's what pushed her into the pit of despair these last few days. Where she never changed out of her pajamas and she didn't wash her hair and she ate ice cream straight out of the carton. She was a pitiful mess who blew it with the best guy who ever could've happened to her.

"I don't want to hang out with you and Harper. You two are sickeningly in love with my asshole brothers." She was still irrationally pissed at West and Lane too. It was totally unfair on her part considering they'd wanted to protect her or whatever, but she couldn't help herself.

The arsonist was still at work. Another fire had been started over the weekend. It was at an old abandoned cabin high up in the mountains above Wildwood, and there was no reason for someone to burn it down with the exception that it was just…there.

That's what she told Josh Bailey when he came around to talk to her. "He didn't want to burn my house down because I lived there," she'd said. "He started the fire because he had the opportunity, and my little house was just…there. I lived on an isolated road. Not many people came out there, and I'd been gone all day. It was the perfect scenario for him."

Josh had agreed, though he still wasn't ruling out the possibility that she'd been targeted. Whatever. What was done, was done. She wasn't going to walk around in fear. This was her hometown, for the love of God. She knew mostly everyone who lived here; most of them she'd known her entire life. She wasn't scared, not of anyone.

What she was scared of though? The possibility that she could lose Tate forever.

This was her moment to start fresh, and she wanted to start with Tate by her side. Tate making her laugh, making her sigh with pleasure, making her feel safe. She didn't want to lose him. She'd give up everything else if she knew it would mean Tate was forever in her life.

But she wasn't sure if he felt the same way.

Delilah tugged on her hair, making Wren yelp. "You need to talk to Tate," Dee said.

"I'd love to. But it's kind of hard to do when he's not even in town." Wren sighed and stared at her lap, clutching her hands together. "He should hate me."

"Please."

"He probably thinks I hate him."

"You'll eventually forgive your brothers. Surely you'll forgive Tate too?" Delilah asked.

"I have to forgive West and Lane. They're my brothers. Family. They were just being their usual overprotective selves."

"I'm guessing Tate was doing the same—the overprotective bit." Delilah tapped Wren on the shoulder, and she turned to meet her friend's gaze. "Isn't it nice to know so many big brawny men are watching over you?"

Wren made a face. "Sort of. It's more annoying than anything else. It's like they don't trust I can make the right decisions."

"More like they don't trust the weirdo who's out there setting fires," Delilah said. "It had nothing to do with you and your supposed inability to function in life. More like they just wanted to make sure you were safe. They care about you. Your brothers love you."

"Yeah." Wren plucked at a loose thread on her faded flannel pajama pants. "I love them too, even though they drive me nuts."

"And what about Tate?" Delilah nudged Wren's shoulder with her own. "I'm guessing your moping around has been over him."

"You already know this." She shook her head and sighed. "I probably blew it with him, huh?"

"Doubtful. He's been on a fire. Not like he's off getting drunk and seeking out other women."

Ugh. She hated the image Delilah just put into her brain. But she knew it wasn't true. Tate had been working the entire time since she last saw him. He wasn't out finding someone else. Hopefully he was still thinking about…her.

A girl could dream, at least.

"Word on the street is that Tate's engine is coming back to Wildwood later today," Delilah said, sending her a look.

Hope lit a bright flame in her chest, making her heart thump. "Don't tease me."

"I'm not. West already told Harper, and she told me." Delilah's gaze swept over Wren, and she wrinkled her nose. "I think you need to go make yourself pretty so you can be at the station to greet him when he arrives."

Wren leapt to her feet. "Does it matter if I look pretty or not? I mean, he shouldn't care if I'm all made up with perfect hair and stuff." If she remembered correctly, he seemed to like her best naked and makeup-free, with her hair a mess. He didn't care if she ate burgers for dinner or ice cream for…every meal. He just seemed to like her for her.

"I'm not saying you need to go glamorize yourself. Just…take a shower. You kind of need one." Delilah held her nose like Wren was stinking up the place, which made her laugh. "Go. Take a shower. Get ready for your man's return home."

By the time Delilah finished her sentence, Wren was already making her way to the bathroom.

TIRED. HUNGRY. DIRTY. *Tired. Starving. Smelly.* Those were the main words that kept repeating themselves in Tate's brain, reminding him that he needed a break in a major way. He'd never been happier to be let go from a fire than he was when he left this one. It had been particularly brutal. He and his crew had covered the day shift, setting backfires to ensure the main fire wouldn't rage out of control in rugged terrain. His muscles ached from all the climbing, and the weather was miserably hot, typical for late August. Worse, they'd had to sleep outside on the rocky ground, which sucked major balls.

He'd tossed and turned through most of those nights, pretending to sleep under the stars, too uncomfortable, his thoughts filled with Wren. He missed her. He wanted to beg for her forgiveness. Figure out a way to earn her forgiveness so she'd give him a second chance. A woman like Wren Gallagher didn't just walk into a man's life every day. She was special. Sweet. Smart. Beautiful. Funny. Sexy. Feisty. And at one point, she'd been his.

He wanted her back.

Once he got home, took a shower, and slept for a solid twelve hours, he would search her out, talk to her, and make her see reason. They belonged together. He missed his little dove, and he had a suspicion she missed him too.

He couldn't blame her for being angry with him, but if she could forgive her bonehead brothers, then she could definitely forgive him too.

"Ah, home sweet home." Tori, one of the firefighters at the station who'd recently changed shifts and was now on his crew, sat up straighter in the passenger seat of the rig as they crossed the Wildwood town limits. She fought for the passenger seat more than any of the others, and he figured she got car sick, though she never admitted it. He noticed everyone else just usually let her have the seat. She was young and tough and a good conversationalist. He enjoyed talking to her while they drove, plus she had a good eye, so she'd spot the fire or the wrecked car or whatever faster than he did. She was a good worker, competent, and she'd shifted over to his crew effortlessly. She was a good fit.

"Glad to be back," Tate said with a sigh as he drove through the little town. He took in the familiar sights, his heart and mind weary as he thought yet again of Wren. He hoped she was okay. He'd heard about the fire the arsonist set that destroyed an abandoned cabin just above Wildwood Lake, and while that wasn't good news, at least nothing happened to Wren.

"Me too. I miss my bed," Tori said.

"I think we all do."

"They're not going to keep us at the station overnight, are they?"

"I don't know. I think everyone's on staff. No other engines have taken off for another fire." He'd had that happen before. Coming home from a fire only to be kept at the station for another week as coverage because they were short an engine. It happened all the time in the height of summer.

"Good." Tori settled back against the seat and gazed out the window. "I just want to go home."

"Me too," he murmured, steering the engine through town, thankful he hit every single—all two of them—green light so he could increase his speed as he drew closer to the station.

It was on the other side of town, near the lake and the surrounding day parks and campgrounds. The pine trees grew tall as they approached the lake, obscuring the water view until they were right upon it. It came as a pleasant surprise every time he saw it. That wide expanse of deep blue, the sandy beaches combined with the rocky shore. The giant hotel that sat on the other side of the lake, tall and grand as the late summer sun shone upon its roof, the US and state flags flapping wildly in the breeze from the rooftop.

He liked this town. More than anything, he liked the people in it. Since moving here, he'd made good friends. He worked with solid people. And he'd met a great woman, one he wanted to keep in his life, if she'd still have him.

The moment he eased up on the brake and turned right onto the fire station driveway, a sense of relief washed over him. They'd made it home safely. They'd need to clean the rig and get everything in order, but then he'd let everyone go home. He'd radioed in to West as they went through town, asking if they were still needed at the station. Thank Christ West had said they were released to go home.

"Isn't that Wren Gallagher?" Tori suddenly asked, causing Tate to jerk on the steering wheel, making the engine sway. She sent him a curious glance. "You okay?"

"Fine," he said gruffly, righting the engine as he tried to find Wren. Ah, hell, and there she was. Sitting on the hood of a car, wearing that same pretty pink dress she had on the night he first saw her naked. Her hair was blowing in the wind. A strand crossed her face, and she brushed it away impatiently, her eyes widening when she saw his engine approach.

Her gaze met his through the windshield, and she waved, a shy smile curving her lush lips.

His heart started to race. She was there for him. She was actually waiting for him to arrive. He thought the best thing that would greet him today would be his bed.

Instead, it turned out to be Wren.

Tate pulled the rig to a stop in front of the garage and turned off the engine, chuckling when Tori threw open the passenger door and exited the vehicle. He thought he was the eager one, but they all spilled off the engine, tired and happy to be on familiar ground.

Slowly he opened the driver's side door to see Wren standing there, smiling up at him. He caught that hint of cleavage that drove him out of his mind, her scent blowing toward him on the breeze, and he'd never seen a better sight.

He emerged from the engine and shut the door before turning to face her. She'd taken a few steps back to give him room, and that nervous smile was still in place.

"Hi," she said, her voice filling him up, reminding him of just how much he'd missed her.

"Hey." He rested his hands on his hips, tilting his head to the side. "Didn't expect to see you here."

"A pleasant surprise, I hope?" she asked, sounding worried.

"The best kind of surprise." His answer caused her smile to grow, and she ducked her head, her hair falling forward and obscuring her face. "What are you doing, Dove?"

She lifted her head, tears shining in her eyes. "I was afraid I'd never hear you call me that again."

"I thought you hated the bird nicknames." He took a step toward her, ignoring the rest of his crew milling about, their loud voices fading to nothing but a faint buzz as he concentrated on Wren. He hated seeing her cry. Hated more that he might be the cause of her tears. "Now you're even crying because of them."

"No." She shook her head, and a watery laugh escaped her. "They're happy tears. I—I missed you, Tate. So much. I'm sorry I shut you out."

He took another step closer. "I'm sorry I didn't tell you the cause of the fire."

Now it was her turn to take a step. "I know why you did it. I just…overreacted. My brothers have been over-protective my entire life and I've always hated it." He touched her face, streaked his thumbs under her eyes to wipe away the dreaded tears that made his heart ache. "But I could never hate you. I know it's happened fast, but I really care about—"

Tate kissed her before she could finish the sentence, swallowing her words, her laughter, the contented sigh that escaped when his tongue tangled with hers. She wrapped her arms around his neck and clung to him, pressing her body against his, and he gripped her hips, setting her away from him and wincing when he saw the smudges on her skirt.

"Got you dirty," he murmured, his gaze never leaving hers.

"I like it when you make me dirty," she said with another sigh, the little smile curling her lips making his cock twitch. Even though he was filthy and hungry and exhausted, he still wanted her.

Had a feeling he'd always want her.

"Hmm, I bet." He kissed her again, unable to resist her lips, though he made sure not to touch her too much. "Come home with me," he murmured against her lips when they broke apart.

"I thought you'd never ask." She leaned in and brushed her lips to his cheek. "I mean it. I don't have a ride."

Tate frowned. "What do you mean?"

"Delilah dropped me off about an hour ago. West was keeping me updated on your progress home." She grinned. "I was kind of scared you'd turn me down."

"Never." He grabbed hold of her and kissed her thoroughly, forgetting all about his dirty clothes and hands, forgetting everything but the taste of Wren's lips and the little sounds of pleasure she made when he swept his tongue inside her mouth. "Now that you're here, I'll never let you go."

"Really?" Her voice squeaked, and she pressed her hands against his chest, her fingers fiddling with the collar of his uniform shirt.

He kissed the tip of her nose. "Really."

Chapter Twenty

WREN SKIMMED HER fingers across Tate's bare chest in lazy circles, first around one nipple, then the other, before running through the small patch of dark hair that was in the middle of his chest. She could touch him like this forever and never get tired of it. He probably wouldn't get tired of it either.

That low, sexy murmur she just heard rumbling in his chest was proof.

They'd been home for hours, and in that time, Tate had taken a shower, with her help. Afterward, they'd called in a pizza order, and she'd given him a blow job while they waited. They ate dinner and hung out, until his wandering hands landed between her legs, and now they were in bed. Naked. After a rather vigorous bout of sex.

"I'm so tired," he practically groaned, his eyes firmly closed. She stared at his thick, dark eyelashes, sort of hating him for a quick moment because he had the eyelashes of her dreams. There was not enough mascara in the world to give her those same results. "You're keeping me awake."

She poked him in the side with her index finger, making him swerve away from her. "I told you already that you don't need to stay awake on my account."

"But you keep touching me."

"So?"

"So someone likes that."

"Someone should just go to sleep," she suggested.

"He can't."

She laid her head back on his warm chest, trying to smother her laughter. "Why not?"

"This is why." He reached for her hand and slipped it under the covers, her fingers brushing against his very hard cock.

"Oh." The laughter died in her throat, and her blood heated. "Um, that's a problem."

"I know." He sighed, gently forcing her fingers to curl around his length. "You need to help me."

"I do, huh?" She started to stroke him very slowly, from root to tip, earning a soft moan for her efforts. "How's that?"

"It's working," he said, his voice tense.

"Good." She kept up the slow pace, pressing her thighs together when he jerked the sheet back and exposed them. She watched in fascination as she continued to stroke him, marveling that he was so big, so thick, and so hard after they'd just had sex—when? Not even twenty minutes ago?

Maybe fifteen.

"You're like the Energizer Bunny," she said.

"I just keep going and going?" He cracked his eyes open and peered up at her.

"Exactly." She released her hold on his cock and cradled his balls. "You really want to do this all over again?"

"With you, it's easy. I think whenever I'm around you, this is going to be a natural state." He pointed down at his erection.

Wren laughed and shook her head. "That's going to be a big problem."

"I know." He sounded so serious. "You know what that means, right?"

"What?"

"That you belong to me." He paused. "And I belong to you."

Her heart threatened to crack wide open and spill all over the place. Oh, she was well on her way to falling in love with this man, if that last declaration wasn't enough already. "That has a nice ring to it," she said, sounding choked up.

Maybe because she was choked up.

He touched her cheek, tilted her face up so their mouths were perfectly aligned. His breath feathered across her lips, and she closed her eyes. "It does, doesn't it?"

Before she could answer him, he kissed her.

That was answer enough.

Have you read the other fun, steamy romances in the Wildwood Series?

Be sure to check out West and Harper's story…

Ignite

As well as Lane and Delilah's story…

Smolder

Available now from Avon Impulse!

About the Author

USA Today bestselling author **KAREN ERICKSON** writes what she loves to read—sexy contemporary romance. Published since 2006, she's a native Californian who lives in the foothills below Yosemite with her husband and three children. She also writes as *New York Times* and *USA Today* bestselling author Monica Murphy. You can find her at www.karenerickson.com.

Give in to your Impulses . . .
Continue reading for excerpts from
our newest Avon Impulse books.
Available now wherever ebooks are sold.

THE VIRGIN AND THE VISCOUNT

A BACHELOR LORDS OF LONDON NOVEL

by Charis Michaels

LOVE ON MY MIND

by Tracey Livesay

HERE AND NOW

AN AMERICAN VALOR NOVEL

by Cheryl Etchison

An Excerpt from

THE VIRGIN AND
THE VISCOUNT
A Bachelor Lords of London Novel
By Charis Michaels

Lady Elisabeth Hamilton-Baythes has a
painful secret. At fifteen, she was abducted by
highwaymen and sold to a brothel. But two days
later, she was rescued by a young lord, a man
she's never forgotten. Now, she's devoted herself
to save other innocents from a similar fate.

Bryson Courtland, Viscount Rainsleigh, never
breaks the rules. Well, once, but that was a
long time ago. He's finally escaped his unhappy
past to become one of the wealthiest noblemen
in Britain. The last thing he needs to complete
his ideal life? A perfectly proper wife.

Bryse.

He had introduced himself as Bryson that night, so long ago, and despite her residual horror, she had clung to the sweet intimacy of that introduction. She'd devoted years of foolish fantasies to guessing whether those close to him referred to him as Bryson or Bryse or perhaps Court . . .

She looked up at him. *Bryse.* And now she knew. Now she was being invited to become one of those people close to him.

Cowardice compelled her to back away and retake her seat. "Forgive me, my lord." She spoke to her knees. "I don't know what to say, and that is a rare circumstance, indeed."

"I would also speak to your aunt," he assured her. "It felt appropriate to suggest the idea of a courtship to you first."

She laughed, in spite of herself. "I'd say so. Unless you wish to court my aunt."

"I wish for you," he said abruptly, and Elisabeth's head shot up. It was almost as if he knew she needed to hear it again, and again, and again.

I wish for you.

He crouched before her chair, spreading his arms, putting

one hand on either side of her chair, caging her in. "How old are you, Elisabeth?" he asked.

"How old do you think I am?" A whisper.

"Twenty-six?" he guessed.

She shook her head. "No. I am the ripe old age of thirty. Far too old to be called upon by a bachelor viscount, rolling in money."

"Or"—he arched an eyebrow—"exactly the right age."

She laughed and finally looked away. And she thought he'd been handsome at nineteen. Her stomach dropped into a dip. She reminded herself to breathe.

"Why me?" she asked, looking out the window. "Why pay attention to *me*?"

His voice was so low she could barely discern the words. "Because I think you'd make an ideal viscountess."

An ideal what? Hope became a living, pulsing thing in her chest. It became her very heart. She fell back in her seat and closed her eyes, but the room still swam before her.

He went on, "You are mature, and intelligent, and poised. And devoted to your charity, whatever it is."

A thread of the old conversation. She sat up, determined to seize it before he could say another thing. "I've just told you what the charity is."

"You spoke in vague generalities that could mean a great many things. I let it go because I hope for more opportunities to learn."

Elisabeth breathed in and out, in and out. She bit her bottom lip again. She watched his gaze hone in on her mouth.

She closed her eyes. "My lord." She took a deep breath.

"Rainsleigh . . . Bryson." She opened her eyes. "If your far-reaching goal is to earn an esteemed spot in London society, you're going about it entirely the wrong way. My charity is . . . unpopular, and no one has ever asked to court me before. It's really not done."

"Why is that?"

Because I have been waiting for you.

The thought floated, fully formed, in her brain, and she had to work to keep her hands from her cheeks, to keep from closing her eyes again, from squinting them shut against his beautiful face, just inches from her own, his low voice, his boldness.

"I'm very busy," she said instead.

"Then I will make haste."

"Is this because of last night? When I . . . challenged your dreadful neighbor?"

The corner of his mouth hitched up. "It did not hurt."

"It's very difficult for me to stand idly by when I hear a person misrepresented."

"And to think I was under the impression that you could barely abide my company. Your defense came as a great surprise."

"Oh . . . I am full of surprises."

"Is that so?" His words were a whisper. He leaned in.

She had the fleeting thought: *Dear God. He's going to kiss me . . .*

An Excerpt from

LOVE ON MY MIND

By Tracey Livesay

Tracey Livesay makes her Avon Impulse
debut with a sparkling and sexy novel about
a woman who will do anything to fulfill her
dreams . . . but discovers that even the best
laid plans can fail when love gets in the way.

Chelsea Grant couldn't tear her gaze away from the train wreck on the screen.

She followed press conferences like most Americans followed sports. The spectacle thrilled her, watching speakers deftly deflect questions, state narrow political positions, or, in rare instances, exhibit honest emotions. The message might be scripted but the reactions were pure reality. If executed well, a press conference could be as engaging and dynamic as any athletic game.

But watching this one was akin to lions in the amphitheater, not tight ends on the football field. Her throat ached, impacting her ability to swallow. She squinted, hoping the action would lessen her visual absorption of the man's public relations disaster.

He'd folded his arms across his chest, the gesture causing the gray cardigan he wore to pull across his broad shoulders. The collar of the black-and-blue plaid shirt he wore beneath it brushed the underside of his stubbled jaw.

When he'd first stepped onto the platform, she'd thought he was going for "geek chic." All he'd lacked were black square frames and a leather cross-body satchel. Now she understood he wasn't playing dress-up. These were his everyday clothes, and as such, they were inappropriate for a press conference, unless he was a lumberjack who'd just won the lottery.

Had someone advised him on how to handle a press conference? No, she didn't think so. *Any* coaching would have helped with his demeanor. The man stared straight ahead. He didn't look at the reporters seated before him. He didn't look into the lenses. He appeared to look over the cameras, like there was someplace else he'd rather be. His discomfort crossed the media plane, and her fingers twitched where they rested next to her iPad on the acrylic conference table.

A female reporter from an entertainment news cable channel raised her hand. "Mr. Bennett?"

The man turned his head, and his gaze zeroed in on the reporter and narrowed into a glare. Chelsea inhaled audibly and leaned forward in her chair. His eyes were thickly lashed and dark, although she couldn't determine their exact color. Brown? Black? He dropped his arms, and his long, slender fingers gripped the podium tightly. The bank of microphones jiggled and a loud piercing sound ripped through the air. He winced.

"How does it feel to be handed the title by David James?" the reporter asked, her voice louder as it came on the tail end of the noise feedback.

The camera zoomed in and caught his pinched expression. "Right now, I feel annoyed," he responded sharply.

"Annoyed? Aren't you honored?"

"Why should I be honored?"

"Because *People Magazine* has never named a non-actor as their sexiest man alive."

"An award based on facial characteristics is not an honor. Especially since I have no control over the symmetry of my features. The National Medal of Technology. The Faraday Medal. The granting of those awards would be a true honor."

The camera zoomed out, and hands holding phones with a smaller version of the man's frustrated image filled the screen. Flashes flickered on the periphery, and he rubbed his brow, like Aladdin begging the genie for the power to disappear.

"How does one celebrate being deemed the most desirable man on the planet?" another reporter asked.

"One doesn't." His lips tightened into a white slash on his face.

"Is there a secret scientific formula for dating Victoria's Secret models? Didn't you used to be engaged to one?" A male reporter exchanged knowing looks with the colleagues around him. A smattering of chuckles followed his question.

"Didn't she leave you for another model six weeks before the wedding?"

"So you're single? Who's your type?"

"What's your perfect first date?"

"Can you create a sexbot?"

Questions pelted the poor man. The reporters had found his weakness: his inability or unwillingness to play the game. Now they would try to get a sound bite for their story teaser or a quote to increase their site's click-through rate. The man drove his fingers through his black hair, a move so quick and natural she knew it was a gesture he repeated often. That, and not hair putty, probably explained the spikiness of the dark strands that were longer on the top, shorter on the sides.

"This has nothing to do with my project," he snapped, then scowled at someone off-camera.

Chelsea glanced heavenward, grateful she wasn't the recipient of that withering look.

An Excerpt from

HERE AND NOW
An American Valor Novel
By Cheryl Etchison

Former Ranger Medic Lucky James feels right at home working long night shifts in the ER, but less so during the day, when his college classes are filled with flirtatious co-eds. When his 19-year-old chem lab partner shows up at his work with dinner for "her Lucky," he quickly enlists the help of Rachel Dellinger, a nurse and fellow third shift "vampire." From there a friendship is born between two people just trying to make it through the night. Neither are living in the past or planning for the future—until one day changes everything.

When the phone kept ringing non-stop and the desk clerk asked her to take a set of scrubs to exam room seven, Rachel didn't think much of it. It was, after all, an ER and she assumed they were for a patient whose clothes were ruined and was in need of something to wear home. She gave a light tap to the exam room door and pushed it opened further, expecting to find someone at least sitting on the exam table and requiring assistance. What she did not expect was to see a fine physical specimen, upright and most certainly able-bodied, whipping his shirt off over his head in one swift, fluid motion. Nor did she expect to be greeted by strong shoulders, a broad muscular back, and narrowed hips.

Holy moly.

This guy was by far the best looking man she'd seen in the flesh in a very long time. Maybe ever. And she hadn't even seen his face.

She clutched the scrubs to her chest and stood silent and tongue-tied, watching, appreciating, as the muscles in his back and arms flexed and strained as he unfastened the leather belt around his waist and released the button. All those finely sculpted muscles worked in unison to create a stunning physical display of power and strength as he shoved his pants to the floor.

Wearing only white crew socks and gray boxer briefs, he turned to face her and she nearly forgot how to breathe. She thought the back was nice? The chest. The abs. The dark trail of hair that began just below his navel and disappeared beneath the waistband of his briefs.

"You could've dropped them on the table and left instead of just standing there."

Her gaze shot upward to see one corner of his mouth lifted in a half smile and as dark brown eyes stared back at her she was immediately struck by the feeling she knew this guy. There was something so familiar about him, but she couldn't quite put her finger on it.

She swallowed hard in an effort to unstick her tongue from the roof of her mouth. "You knew I was standing here?"

Instead of answering, he simply held out his hand, his eyes flicking to the scrubs she held in a stranglehold against her chest before lifting to meet hers once again.

"How?" She relaxed her grip, felt the blood rush back to her fingertips as she placed the scrubs in his hand. "How did you know?"

"Spatial awareness," he said taking the clothes from her and immediately tossing the shirt onto the gurney. "That and you knocked on the door before you came in." He flashed that half smile again before stepping into the pants and tying the drawstring. "Thanks for the clothes, Rachel. I can handle it from here."

Immediately she looked down to see if he'd read the name from her badge, only to realize her crossed arms were covering her ID. Clearly, he knew her. So she looked harder this time, doing her best to ignore the chest—and abs and arms—and focus on his face. As she mentally stripped away the disheveled hair, the heavy scruff covering his face, the laugh lines around his eyes, the earlier feelings of lust were replaced by a sinking feeling in the pit of her stomach.

There was little doubt the man standing in front of her was the one and only Lucky James.